Hot Assets

DALLAS DEBUTANTES: CARMICHAEL TRILOGY

CYNTHIA D'ALBA

D1603299

Riante Romance
Second Edition

Foreword

Hot Assets was originally published in May 2022 as part of the Rescued Dog Collection. It was available for three weeks, and hasn't been published since.

This is a second edition of this book. It has been reedited, and extended with added scenes,

The characters and the story have remained the same.

I hope you enjoy this first book in the new Carmichael Trilogy.

Copyright

Cover Artist: Steven Novak
Editor: Delilah Devlin

One

I bolted upright in bed, jarred awake. What had woken me up? I pressed my hand against my chest, my heart slamming against it as though trying to pound its way out. Blood thundered in my ears. The darkness and silence of the room only served to accentuate my heavy breathing. I glanced around my bedroom trying to determine what had woken me, but nothing appeared out of place or unusual.

Glancing toward the ceiling, I read the time reflected there. Two a.m. Fine. I still had three more hours I could sleep, and I needed every one of them. With a sigh of relief, I slipped back into my sheets, but before I could wiggle my butt into the mattress and shut my eyes, my cell phone began to ring and vibrate on the table. With a groan, I reached for it, mentally preparing myself for something awful because everyone knew only bad news came in the middle of night...or the random obscene call. However, since I'd gotten rid on a landline and only used cell, those middle-of-the-night calls had stopped, and I can't say I missed them.

Out of habit, I read the caller ID. It was my elderly next-door neighbor. It was then I realized I'd missed a prior call from her, which was probably what had woken me.

"Lillian?" I croaked into my phone. I cleared my throat. "What's wrong?"

"I fell, and I can't move." Lillian's voice was reedy and weak, barely audible. "Help me."

"Of course," I replied as I slipped from my warm sheets. "I'll be right there."

I slipped on the jeans and long-sleeve T-shirt I'd been wearing last night. I was aware the shirt bore a definite spaghetti sauce splotch from dinner, but whatever, I didn't have time, or want to take time, to find something else to wear. After shoving my feet into a pair of slippers, I retrieved Lillian's house key from a drawer in the entry hall table.

I don't usually have the keys of neighboring houses, but Lillian Branson had given me one so I could water her plants while she'd been away on her three-week around-the-world tour. Lillian had been my neighbor for a couple of years. She'd always been a healthy, active senior citizen, always on the go. She belonged to a group of similar-minded seniors who loved to travel, especially on cruises. She'd arrived home ten days ago with what she'd termed a "bad cold," and had refused to see a doctor for something so minor.

Now, as I rushed out of my house and across our

adjoining lawns, a tingle of guilt filled my belly. Should I have pushed Lillian harder to see a doctor? Maybe, but we were neighbors, not relatives and sometimes I had a tendency to stick my nose into other people's business, especially family. But my sister was a doctor. I could have asked Brooke to stop by and take a look at Lillian. Now, that would have made Lillian madder than a wet hen, but with her only family being a grandson whom I'd never met, or even seen visit Lillian in all the time we'd been neighbors, I felt someone—i.e. me—should keep an eye on her. I realized I hadn't done a good job at that.

I unlocked the front door and let myself in. I turned toward the alarm panel to deactivate it but I was surprised to find the house alarm already off. That was very unlike Lillian. I knew she used her alarm at night without fail.

"Lillian?" I shouted.

"In here," she called weakly, followed by a bark from Baxter, her mixed-breed rescue dog. Baxter, who weighed close to eight pounds but believed himself closer to eighty, was always at Lillian's side. Her protector angel. Baxter traveled everywhere with Lillian. If Baxter wasn't invited, odds were, Lillian wasn't going.

I followed the faint voice and barking to the kitchen where I found Lillian sprawled on the floor. Her head had a small gash. Fresh blood trickled down the side of her face. Baxter's head rested on Lillian's chest. It was only when I knelt beside her that Baxter's head lifted.

"Oh, my goodness, Lillian. What happened?"

"I feel like such a ninny. You know I've had that cough for a while. I got to coughing my fool head off and came downstairs to get some water. The rug slipped as I was reaching for the glass and down I went."

I heard my sister's voice in my head warning me not to try to get Lillian up but to call for help instead. Broken hips in women of Lillian's age were all too common.

"Sit still. You have a small cut on your head. Let me grab a towel." I stood and walked around her island to get a clean dishtowel. As I did, I couldn't help but notice the dirty glasses and plates piled in the sink. Lillian was one of the tidiest people I'd ever met. She hated disorder, so having dinner dishes in the sink and not in the dishwasher was totally out of character for her.

I found a towel and hurried back to where I'd left her on the floor. I pressed the clean material to her head. "Other than the headache from hitting your head, where else are you hurting?"

"My left hip. I landed on it when I fell." She clicked her tongue as she shook her head. "I am so clumsy."

I felt Lillian's hip, but I'm pretty sure I wouldn't know a broken hip unless a bone jabbed my hand, but I felt like I needed to do something. "Is someone else here?"

"No. Just me."

"Hmm, well I noticed your alarm was off when I came in."

Lillian groaned when I touched her hip, and her gaze shifted away. "Nobody here. I'm here by myself. That's why I had to call you." Tears gathered in her eyes.

She was lying to me. That was as obvious as the dirty dishes in her sink. Why did she feel the need to lie about company?

"Yeah, I can't get you up. I'm sorry," I said. "My money's on either a dislocated or broken hip." I squeezed her shoulder in sympathy. "Sorry, hon, but I've got to call an ambulance." I braced myself for an argument since Lillian is one of the most independent women I knew. When Lillian only nodded her head in agreement, I knew I'd made the right call this time.

After I called 9-1-1 and explained the situation, I knew we'd have a wait of unknown duration for an ambulance. I tried to help her settle into a more comfortable position, but the reality was no position was great. I joined her on the hardwood and crossed my ankles.

"Well, this is a fine mess you've gotten us into," I said in my best Laurel and Hardy imitation.

She chuckled and then grimaced. "I know." She glanced over at me. "I am so sorry to get you out of bed in the middle of the night."

"Hey, stop that. That's what neighbors are for," I assured her. "I really don't mind."

Heavy footfalls boomed from the entryway. My

attention and gaze jolted from my injured neighbor toward the noise. I hadn't heard the wail of an ambulance siren, and frankly, I'd be shocked if one had gotten here that quickly unless it was just one block away.

A man dressed in dark jeans, a button-up oxford, and a jacket barged into the kitchen. I realized that in my haste to get into the house and to Lillian, I might have left the front door standing open. Wow, that was a dumb mistake. Panic seized my throat and my breath for good reason.

My neighborhood was a recognized Dallas historical area that my great-grandparents had founded. Carmichael Gardens was a small city that Dallas had engulfed as it had grown and expanded over the years. This small incorporated area was comprised mostly of old craftsman homes, many over a hundred years old.

Lillian and I both lived in totally refurbished homes in the classically historical neighborhood. While many of the houses had undergone renovation and updating necessary to bring them back to their stately beauty, others remained in poor condition, with the owners lacking the funding to do the required upkeep. Recently, my family trust, the Carmichael Foundation, had taken on grant funding to help these owners.

Inside our fenced and gated neighborhood enclave, there was a false sense of security because neighbors watched out for neighbors. Outside our walls, however, the crime rates were higher than the average for other Dallas neighborhoods. Was the scruffy-looking man one of the criminal elements I needed to be worried about?

The man standing in Lillian's kitchen was tall and broad-shouldered. His wavy, chestnut-colored hair was disheveled, as though he'd run his fingers through it recently. A heavy stubble covered his cheeks and circled a pair of thick lips that were currently pulled into a tight line.

"Get out," I ordered in my best don't-fuck-with-me voice that usually made my employees sit up and take notice. I pointed toward the direction he'd arrived.

I might have been anxious, but Baxter sure wasn't. He raced toward to the man with a wiggly tail and excited jumps and yips.

"Hey, boy," the stranger said with a quick pat on the dog's head before he continued to advance toward us. Seated on the floor, I recognized our vulnerable position. I had no way to protect or fend off an attack, but I would protect Lillian the best I could.

"Lillian, are you okay?" he asked in a gentle voice. He squatted beside her. "What happened?"

Lillian smiled at the stranger even though she was obviously in pain. Whoever he was, she and Baxter knew him so I could let go of my attack dog persona.

"I'll be fine," Lillian said with a tsk. "I had a little slip and fall."

"Do I need to call an ambulance?" he asked with a concerned frown.

His question rubbed me the wrong way. What did he think I was doing here? Working a jigsaw puzzle? "I've got it covered, Mr...?"

"Noles. Zack Noles. I knew you lived in the area, Andi. I just hadn't had time to come by your house."

I only remembered one Zack Noles and he was part of my past...my long-ago past. How common was that name? Had I ever met another man with that name? I met a lot of people in my position as CEO of my family's philanthropic foundation, but I'm sure I would have remembered him if we'd met through my job.

I studied him closer—penetrating gray eyes. I only knew one person with those eyes. My heart skipped a few beats.

"Zack lives across the street," Lillian said, interrupting my thoughts. "In the old Skaggs place."

I knew the house. While it was on the historical preservation list, the structure was pretty much in terrible shape and was an eyesore to the area. Recently, to my relief, I'd noticed some renovation taking place. Ceramic tile and backerboard had been delivered last week. The Carmichael Family Foundation had taken on the renovation of Carmichael Gardens in memory of my father's family and the source of most of the family fortune. I had wondered if I was seeing one of the grants in action.

The whoop of an ambulance siren and a flashing red light announced the arrival of the ambulance. I felt like I could finally take a breath. People who knew what to do were finally here.

"I'll go meet the ambulance so they know they're at the right house. Is that okay with you, Lillian?" I asked.

"Of course. Zack will stay with me."

My gaze flicked between my injured neighbor and the man. He felt so familiar. When I tried to think about Zack Noles from college, my brain threw up a concrete wall, as I'd instructed it to. "I'll be right back. Come on, Baxter. Let's get you out of the way," I said, picking up the tiny dog.

The paramedics were coming up the walk when I got to the front door...which was still open. I gestured for them to follow me. The male paramedic was tall, white, and at least fifty pounds overweight. The other was a petite, attractive Hispanic with caring eyes and a face that lit up at the site of Zack Noles.

"Detective Noles," she purred. "Haven't seen you in a while." She grinned. "Too long, actually."

Noles chuckled. "Good to see you, Anita. You too, Lonnie."

Lonnie, the male paramedic, said, "This ain't your shift, Detective. Whatcha doing here?" He eyed Lillian. "Break-in?"

Noles frowned. "No break-in. Lillian fell." He eyed the woman on the floor. "There was no break-in...isn't that right, Lillian? You slipped and fell?"

"That's right. Just silly old me falling," Lillian replied.

Again, something felt off, like Lillian wasn't telling the whole truth. I again wondered about the dirty dishes in the sink. There were too many for just Lillian, but she'd said she was alone. However, that didn't mean someone hadn't been here earlier.

"And," Detective Noles continued, "I suspect she fell off the stepstool." He pointed to a white two-step stool sitting crooked. "Have I got that right, Lillian?"

She laughed nervously. "You caught me. I knew you were a sharp detective."

I frowned. That wasn't what Lillian had told me. "What makes you think she fell off the stool?"

"Easy." He held up one finger. "That stool should be way over there in that corner."

When he raised a second finger while speaking, I sneaked a peek at his ring finger—his naked ring finger.

"And second, Lillian has been trying to ignore the out-of-place stool when I know it's driving her crazy."

I'd been Lillian's next-door neighbor for three years, and this guy had been here for what? A couple of months? How could he know so much about her and her habits?

The two paramedics squatted beside Lillian and began to take vital signs. Zack and I stepped over to the side.

"How do you know Lillian?" I asked.

"She's a neighbor. I like to meet all my neighbors."

I arched an eyebrow—a feat that'd taken a lot of time in a mirror to perfect. "I'm your neighbor, and you haven't been over to my house to meet me."

"When I looked up who lived there, I realized we'd already met."

My heart began to race. He was studying me, like a wolf eyeing a bunny for dinner. His gray eyes twinkled under an arched brow. His gorgeous brown hair with its unruly waves. His massively large hands. I remembered it all, but I didn't want to. I didn't want him to believe I'd been fantasizing about him for the past thirteen years.

"Have we?" I asked, hoping to stall, hoping to give myself time to catch my breath and slow my runaway heart.

His response was the smile of someone who knew something others didn't...the smile of a man who knew me intimately.

I turned toward Lillian and the medics. They loaded her onto the ambulance gurney for transport.

"Andi." Lillian waved me over. She grabbed my hand and held tight. "Promise me you'll take care of Baxter. He's very valuable. Promise me you'll protect him."

I squeezed her hand. "Of course I will, Lillian. Don't worry about him at all."

"No, I need you to promise me." She squeezed my hand with surprising and unexpected strength. "Promise me that no one else will take him from you. Promise you'll keep him until I get home."

"I promise," I said, dragging fingers across my chest in an X. "I cross my heart I will take care of Baxter. You just need to focus on getting better."

The older woman relaxed against the gurney. "Thank you."

"I'm happy to have Baxter as a houseguest," I assured her. What I didn't add was the word *temporary,* as in this being a temporary arrangement. I'd never had a house pet. We'd had horses that had lived on someone else's ranch, but never a pet in in our house. Still, I'd promised her, so I felt obligated to care for him.

After the ambulance left, I turned toward Zack. "Would it do any good to pretend I don't remember you?" I asked with a sigh.

He chuckled. His smile released a bevy of butterflies in my stomach, but it always had. "Hmm, nope." He cleared his throat and began to sing. "Texas fight, Texas fight. And..." He sang the entire University of Texas fight song, which stirred up emotions and memories I'd thought long buried deep.

"How are you doing Zack Noles, semi-famous Texas Longhorn quarterback?"

He bowed. "Very well, Ms. Carmichael." His eyebrows arched. "Semi-famous?" He grabbed at his chest. "Damn, woman. That hurt."

Of course, I remembered every minute of every hour we'd spent together. Our time together, including our one and only one-night stand, had been magical. I'd convinced myself that my fairy-tale feelings toward him and about him couldn't be real, and even if it had been real, we'd been young. When the time had come to make the hard decisions about my future, I'd walked away, convinced that kind of fire couldn't last a lifetime. I'd comforted myself by saying I'd experienced a love like few people ever had and I needed to be satisfied with that.

Zack had changed during the intervening years. He'd filled out. Now, he had the body of a man, not a muscular jock, not that I didn't think he probably still had some nice muscles under a jacket that pulled across his shoulders. Plus, back at UT, he'd kept his hair very short. He'd let it grow out. The sexy waves with the touch of silver at the temples didn't look much like the hair of the boy from Austin. Under heavy, dark eyebrows, his eyes bore deep-crinkled laugh lines. His nose had a slight bump that was new to me. Probably a break from his NFL days. A scar I didn't remember cut a tiny groove into the left side of his forehead. But even through the scruff, I could see that dimple in his chin. Yeah, my tongue might have played around in that dimple a time or two. But his luscious lips hadn't changed. Even back in college, he'd known what to do with them. I could only imagine what he'd learned since then. Studying him, jet streams of lust rocked through me.

Thirteen years ago, during a birthday night out with my sisters, I'd met Zack. I felt the sparks between us then, much as I was tonight.

Two

T hirteen Years Ago
         University of Texas, Austin

"Happy Birthday to you," sang seven of our best friends.

My sisters and I—all triplets—were turning twenty-two in five days. However, by then, all of us would have gone our separate ways home to our families for Christmas break. Yeah, sometimes having a birthday on December twentieth wasn't so great. Having two fairly identical sisters made up for that. Our parents had always been great about making sure our birthday was a special day set aside just for us. No birthday slash Christmas presents ever. But it could be difficult to throw a December birthday party without Christmas sneaking in, either in the color scheme or the fresh flowers.

All my life, it has driven me crazy when people asked, "Isn't it awful to have a birthday so close to Christmas," and I want to shout, "I don't know! It's all I've ever known." But I thought what bugged me most about that question was the implied opinion that there was something wrong with a December birthday. Like I said, it's all my sisters and I have ever known, and as far as I was aware, none of us was bothered by our birthday's location on a calendar.

Yeah, I was one of three. Mom must have still been high on drugs when she named us in alphabetical birth order. Andrea, Brooke, and Claudia. Yes, kind of corny, but as the oldest of the group, having my name start with an A reinforced my maturity...all ten minutes before Brooke and thirty minutes before Claudia. As the oldest sister, it was my job never to let them forget I held the power.

I glanced around at my sisters. Both wore bright smiles and sparkling eyes. Our closest sorority sisters had insisted on throwing us a small party after winter finals before we headed home for the holidays. Since Dad would send the plane for us tomorrow and we didn't have to make the long drive from Austin to Dallas, we were happy to hang around, especially for a party in our honor.

When we told our parents that we were hanging around Austin for an extra night so our friends could throw us a birthday party, they'd insisted on providing the cakes, and I suspected picked up the bar tab as well. Each of us had gotten our own cake. Three cakes—Italian cream for Claudia, white with white buttercream icing for Brooke, and red velvet for me. Each cake held twenty-two lit candles with Happy Birthday scrawled across it.

Looking at the smoke the sixty-six lit candles produced, I joked, "I'm surprised we don't set off the fire alarms."

"No kidding," Brooke said with a loud laugh.

"And the parents came through again," Claudia added, gesturing to the three cakes.

My sisters and I sat with seven of our closest friends around a large table on the uppermost level of the Orange Cactus. Without a doubt, this was my favorite bar and this was my favorite level. Of course, most of the time, this level was packed wall to wall with UT students, but so many had already hit the road that the place was only slightly crowded. Reserving the Eagle's Nest for a private event, like tonight's, took some planning.

"Okay, ladies, which of you thought to reserve the Eagle's Nest?" I asked as I sliced into my red velvet cake.

My sorority sister, Dana, raised her hand and waggled her fingers. "That would be me."

"When?" Claudia asked. "It had to be some time ago."

I nodded in agreement with Claudia.

"January."

Claudia slammed her hand on the table. "January? Eleven months ago?"

Dana laughed. "Yep."

"And that's why she's president of every club she belongs to," Pamela said. "No one can organize like Dana."

Dana shrugged. "It's my anal-retentiveness."

My actual sister, Brooke, wrapped her arm around Dana's shoulders and hugged her. "You'll make a great doctor."

Dana shimmied her shoulders. "You and me, babe. We're so going to rock med school."

Brooke agreed with a nod. "They'll never know what hit them." She and Dana tapped wine glasses. "To my future roomie."

The sound of heavy feet on the steps leading up to the Eagle's Nest caught everyone's attention, and we turned en masse to see what was happening. Three waiters approached our table, each carrying a champagne bucket and stand. A waitress trailed behind with a tray of champagne flutes.

"What's this?" Claudia asked.

"Champagne from the gentlemen at the bar," the lead waiter said. "They said to tell the birthday girls happy birthday."

All ten of us leaned over the railing to look for the guys who'd sent three bottles of champagne. At the bar, a line of guys waved up at us and threw a few air kisses before lifting their beer mugs in a toast. Brooke, Claudia, and I waved and blew kisses back while shouting down, "Thank you, guys."

I recognized one of the guys at the bar as Sandy's boyfriend.

I heard Claudia asking Sandy about him.

"Isn't he a sweetie?" Sandy waved over the railing. "Hi, honey! Thanks for the champagne." She blew him a kiss and said, "Big reward later."

The rest of us chuckled because we all knew

exactly what his big reward was going to be, and if the grin on his face was any indication, he did too.

Our ten flutes were filled with champagne.

"Happy Birthday to the bestest triplets I know," Sandy said, lifting her glass in the air.

Do the math. Three bottles of champagne divided by ten very thirsty ladies would leave how much in the bottles? That's right. We went through those bottles lightning quick.

"I think we should order more champagne," Claudia whispered to me.

"Duh," I said with a roll of my eyes. "Do it."

Before we could order, loud stomps on the stairs forecast the arrival of the guys from downstairs, led by Sandy's boyfriend.

"Hello, ladies," Rick, Sandy's boyfriend, said. "Can we join you?"

I glanced around the table and didn't see much opposition.

"And we brought champagne," one of the guys told us and each of the ten guys held up a bottle of champagne.

"Well, in that case, come on," I said.

Chairs began to shift around, and a sexy hunk pulled up a chair up between me and Claudia, but I noticed immediately his attention was on me.

He blasted me a laser-hot smile. "Hey gorgeous. I'm Zack Noles."

Right, like I wouldn't know the team quarterback and well-known playboy on campus.

I returned his smile. "Hello, Zack. I'm Andrea Carmichael, but my friends call me Andi."

He took my hand and kissed my fingers. "Then I'll call you Andi since I want to be a very close friend."

Impossible as it may seem, he scooted his chair even closer to me; close enough his denim-cover thigh rested against mine. Heat radiated from him while his scent—soap and a spicy cologne—wrapped around me.

"I've seen you around campus," he continued.

"Really? And you never spoke."

"I know when someone is out of my league, and honey, you are out of every guy's league."

I tossed my hair over my shoulder with a laugh. "That's a little exaggerated, don't you think? Besides, whenever I've seen you around campus, there was always a girl or two hanging onto you. So don't give me your fake, insecure ego, Zack. You have no problem with confidence."

He chuckled. "So, you think I have an ego?"

"How could you not? Nobody can be a potential first-round draft pick and not have an ego."

"First-round draft pick? You think so?"

I nodded and added, "Unless you screw up something between now and then, and I believe you're smarter than that."

Our conversation meandered for the next hour or so. I enjoyed talking to Zack. He was smart with a wicked sense of humor.

Conversations flowed around us, but we stayed in

our own little pocket and didn't engage with anyone else. But then I became aware of movement and realized the party was breaking up. It'd been fun, but honestly, I was tired. I'd put in some late nights this week. Plus, the plane would be here for Claudia, Brooke, and me at ten, and I still had packing to do.

Zack stood when I stood. "Thank you, Zack. You made an enjoyable night even more so."

"When do you leave for home?"

"We fly to Dallas tomorrow, and to tell you the truth, I haven't begun to pack. Are you headed home also?"

He nodded. "Wish I had a plane coming for me," he said with a chuckle. "I'm driving home. I'll head out tomorrow." He took my hand. "Tonight was great. I'd like to do it again."

I thought about Henry Thaxton. We were broken up—no reason I couldn't give Zack my number and see what happened.

"Give me your phone," I said. I tapped in my name and phone number and then shot a text to myself so I'd have his number. "There. You have my number. Since I rarely answer phone calls from unknown numbers, I sent myself a text so I'd have your number. That work?"

He smiled, and my heart quivered.

"That's works great. Do you need a ride home?"

"I have my car. You can walk me to it if you want."

"I definitely want."

Claudia hadn't moved. Brooke was doing her usual interrogation of the guy sitting with Claudia. That always made me laugh. When it became clear Claudia was not coming home with us right then, I said, "Don't stay out too late. We have an early flight in the morning.

"Thanks, Mom," Claudia said with heavy sarcasm. "Don't forget to give me my allowance for the week."

I just laughed.

As we walked down from the top level to the ground, Zack's hand warmed the small of my back. *Warmed*...What an understatement. The heat from his large hand burned through my shirt and heated my core, making me want to press back against his palm.

Then, to amp my temperature up a few hundred more degrees, he laced his fingers through mine as we passed through the main floor and outside to the parking lot. I don't have petite hands, but Zack had a massive paw. His fingers wrapped around mine in a possessive touch. Flash fires rushed through my body. Lust bloomed in my chest so thick I could hardly breathe.

This response was not something I'd ever experienced. Sure, I'd been aroused by men. I wasn't an innocent virgin. I'd been everywhere on the field—so to speak—except homerun. So no one had actually put his penis inside me, but that was just a technicality, right? I'd never met a man I wanted to get that intimate, until tonight and Zack Noles. My overwhelming need to touch, and be touched, shook me to my core.

"This is me," I said, stepping up to a newer Mustang.

"Are you okay to drive?" His brows furrowed. "I can drive you home."

"I appreciate your concern, but I'm okay. Plus, I don't have that far to go." I placed my hand flat on his chest. "Thank you for, well, keeping me company."

He leaned in. "I hate the timing. I'd love to see you more. Take you out, but..." He dragged his finger down my cheek. "With the bowl game coming up and you leaving campus for Christmas..." He shrugged.

"I understand," I said, and I did. Texas was headed to the Sugar Bowl in New Orleans. It was a huge game, and Zack wanted to go to the NFL Draft this spring. This game was critical, not only for Texas's final ranking but also as a showcase for Zack's talents. Opportunities like the NFL didn't come along for every college athlete. Most would never see a dime from the pro ranks.

His finger trailed along my jaw. "I'll see you in the spring, right?"

"Sure. I'll be here." I forced a smile. "Last semester before being booted into adulthood."

He smiled, and my heart flopped over and died. He was too handsome and too sexy. His beautiful gray eyes twinkled when he looked at me. What he did to me with only a finger told me he could be dangerous to my very carefully planned future. But then the worst thing happened. He kissed me, and my world spun off its axis and I wasn't sure I'd ever be the same.

"Have a good game on New Year's Day," I said as I forced myself off his lips.

"Are you coming?" His voice held such hope, but I shook my head.

"I won't be there, but I'll be watching." I couldn't stop myself from leaning in and kissing him again. "Go kick some ass." I slid into the driver's seat and then looked up at this gorgeous man and said, "Merry Christmas."

He didn't call during the Christmas break. I didn't really expect him to, but that didn't mean I wasn't a tad disappointed. I accepted that I was just a girl he'd met at the Orange Cactus before Christmas break. He had more important people to impress than me.

Three

N ew Year's Day arrived, and with it, the Sugar Bowl game. My sisters and I traditionally held a party for our friends on that day, and this year was no different. We made sure to provide the traditional Southern dishes of black-eyed peas, turnip greens, ham, and cornbread to give them all the inside track on health and wealth for the new year. But there were also dips and chips, brisket sandwiches, barbeque beans, potato salad, and desserts galore. Mom and Dad typically went to their own parties leaving the house to us and our guests...and also a team of catering staff. It seemed to work well for all.

Multiple televisions throughout the house played the different bowl games. Friends came and brought other friends. The party filled the downstairs and flowed out onto the patio and pool deck. The pool wasn't open, of course. It could have been since the pool is heated, but the sisters and I decided last year's toss in the deep end wasn't going to be an option this year.

I went to the kitchen to refill my iced tea and found my sister Claudia with a huge grin on her face. She was putting water into a vase of flowers.

"Let me guess," I said. "Another bouquet of flowers from your mysterious suitor?"

She looked at me and winked. "Not mysterious at all. Just not ready to put him through the sisters' scrutiny."

I looked aghast and slammed my hand to my chest. "What? Me and Brooke? Analyze, scrutinize, and give our loving opinions of any new guy?" Of course, that's what we'd do. If it were me and a new guy, it'd be her and Brooke doing the same. Sisters watched out for each other and triplets might be more protective. We would never stand by and let some guy take advantage.

"Andi?" Brooke called through the house intercom.

"What?"

"You've got company."

I looked at Claudia with a frown. "Ah, yeah. We've got company in every corner of the house. Let me go see what's going on."

I left Claudia in the kitchen with the staff were working our party and headed to the foyer. To my surprise, Henry Thaxton stood there. Now, Henry and I had a complicated history. We'd met our freshman year at orientation. Henry had been cute and funny—a total charmer. We'd dated off and on through our first three years of college. We'd been good companions and great dates, but we'd never stepped over the line into lovers. I couldn't put my finger on why not. I'm sure he would have jumped on that opportunity, but then, I'd found most guys would. I was the holdout. I always felt something was missing. I didn't know what, and I couldn't even explain what I meant. I only knew he wasn't the one.

I hadn't heard from him since he'd broken it off with me in November. I suppose I hadn't been all that surprised when we'd split. Henry had a history of breaking up with me before any occasion that might require a gift. I got it. He was from a middle-class family who struggled to pay his college bills while they still had three other children in Dallas public schools. I'd thought he was probably embarrassed, thinking I'd expect some fancy, expensive gift since I was raised by parents who were in the top one percent of the top one percent. In other words, my folks were loaded. My folks, not me. But I'd spent my life around money. He hadn't. People could be intimidated by that, and I always believed that'd been his problem.

I remembered his first visit to my parents' home. His discomfort had been evident on his face. His conversation skills—one of his best qualities—had dried up at the door. He hadn't stayed long. Now, he usually came around for our New Year's Day party. I wasn't sure if I'd see him this year, but here he was.

"Henry. This is a surprise."

He raked his fingers through his brown, longish hair. "Is it okay that I came by?"

I laughed and pulled him through the door. "Of course, it is."

"So, you don't hate me?"

I scoffed. "I do not. Don't be ridiculous." I linked my arm with his and started leading him to where I knew a group of his fraternity brothers were watching the games. "I'm always glad to see a friend." I pulled him to a stop. "And I do consider you a friend."

I heard his sigh of relief. "Thanks, Andi. You're a great person, but..."

"We aren't meant to be more than friends," I finished for him. "Come with me. I know where a group of your friends are hanging out. Drinks and food are in the dining room or kitchen. You know to make yourself at home."

I left him with his buddies and found my sisters huddled together with a group of our sorority sisters.

"You'll never guess who I just left in the den."

"Henry Thaxton," my friend Pamela said. "Brooke told us. Is he wanting you to take him back?"

"Nope. He's here for the party."

"Are you okay with that?" Missi asked. "Seems a little rude to crash a party at your ex's house."

I laughed. "I'm fine with it. You all know we weren't the love match of our class. I think it's probably good that we've split now. This last semester will be busy with classes and preparations to move to Connecticut."

"I can't believe you're leaving Texas," Pamela said. "I never thought I'd see the Carmichael triplets leave the state of Texas."

"One of us is staying put," Brooke said, who was attending medical school at Baylor.

"Well, I'm excited," Dee said. "I've dreamed of going to Harvard my whole life. The only thing that would make it perfect was if Andi was going with me."

I shook my head. "I think it'll be good for all of us. Besides, think of it as unleashing the power of the Carmichael triplets on the rest of the world."

Our friends laughed, and I hoped I was right.

Texas lost their post-season bowl, so students weren't much into the party mood going back to campus after the holidays. That was fine with me. I was ready to hit those books.

When February rolled around, I confess I was surprised I hadn't heard from Zack Noles. He'd left me the impression he'd be calling, but maybe we hadn't connected like I'd thought we had. Plus, that Sugar Bowl loss was a tough pill for the team to swallow since they'd been favored by more than a touchdown. I didn't know anything about the NFL draft and how players were assessed, so I didn't know if the loss had damaged Zack's chances. I hoped not, but what did I know?

By the middle of March, our baseball team was living up to all their preseason hype. LSU came to town, ready to dethrone us It was a battle on the field, with both teams displaying the talent to take them into the post-season playoffs. However, in the ninth inning, one of our guys hit a grand slam home run, sealing the victory. I'd gone to the game with Brooke, who was a huge baseball nut, and Claudia, after we'd finally gotten her lips separated from Rex's, and that was only because he had an out-of-town hockey game.

Quiet, studious, Brooke became a whole different person in the stands...yelling at the umpire, jeering at the opposing team, cheering on our team loudly. I kept wondering where Brooke hid this crazy, outgoing, side of herself.

Claudia cheered, but it was obvious her heart wasn't into it. She'd thought about flying to Rex's game, but had decided to spend a little time with her sisters since she'd barely seen us since Christmas.

When the last Longhorn player touched home plate, we packed up our seats and purses and headed to the Orange Cactus. The game had started in the late afternoon, so it was close to seven when we got to the bar. We lucked into three stools at the bar and ordered food before the crowd hit. Good thing, too, since ten minutes later, the bar was standing room only. I swear, the walls were bulging with celebrating students. The entire place was rowdy and ready to party.

Forty-five minutes after the game, the baseball players entered to high-fives and cheers that rang above an already deafening noise level. My heart fell to my knees when I saw Zack coming in with a group of student athletes. His gaze roamed around the room as the throng of athletes and their fans made their way toward the end of the bar where I sat.

My hands shook as I lifted my beer to take a sip. There was a mirror behind the bottles of liquor at the bar which gave me a view of what was happening behind me without me having to turn around. Of course, both of my sisters whirled around, so it wasn't hard to figure who I was.

I felt his heat as it penetrated my soul.

"Princess," he said in my ear, sending an army of chills down my spine.

I stiffened my back and turned toward him, ready to send him on his way. Men didn't promise to call and then not follow through. That was a boy's action. But his killer smile, twinkling eyes, dimpled chin, and deadly charm had me melting on my stool. Dammit.

"Have we met?" I asked in a rather snotty tone.

He laughed, and I felt the electrical jolt rush through me. "I'm sorry I haven't called," he whispered in my ear. "After the game, well, my life got crazy. Seem like every time I went near a phone, it was an agent wanting to talk to me. I've spent a lot of time with Coach talking about my future, not to mention I had some classes to get down. But that doesn't mean I haven't thought of you."

I scoffed. "Sure, you have." I rolled my eyes.

He took my hand between his two hands. "I'm

sorry. I know you won't believe this, but I have called. You never answered."

Pulling my phone out of my pocket, I said, "No messages."

"That's because I didn't leave one." He edged closer until his chest was pressed against my side. "There are things I want to say to you, things only for your ears. Things I didn't want to leave on a voice mail."

I turned to fully face him. "Fine. I' here. What is it you want to tell me?"

He shook his head. "Not here. Not like this." He was still holding my hand, which he lifted to his lips. "Come with me."

"Where?"

"My house. Come home with me."

I admit...I was conflicted. Ninety percent of me wanted to leap from the stool. However, ten percent didn't trust him not to hurt me. Not that he would do anything nefarious. I was concerned about my heart.

But my heart overruled my logic and I nodded. Leaning over to Brooke, who was seated between me and Dee, I said, "I'm headed out. I'll see you at home."

Brooke's head whipped around, saw Zack, and then she nodded. "Be safe."

I knew my sister. If she could have, she would have whipped a condom out of her purse and handed it to me. But Zack wasn't a newbie at this sex thing. I assumed he would know what to do.

Hell, I hoped he knew what he was doing because I sure didn't. I'd messed around with guys, given head a couple of times, had a guy's hand down my pants a few times, but that was it. I'd never actually had sex, or as Brooke called it, *intercourse.* I assumed that was why Zack wanted me to come home with him. How embarrassing would it be if I'd misread the entire situation.

He held my hand as we exited the bar. As I'd remembered, his hands were massive and strong. The heat from his fingers radiated up my arm and then then throughout the rest of my body.

"Do you have a car?" he asked.

I shook my head. "I rode here with Brooke. Is that a problem?"

He led me to his truck. "Not a problem. If you decide you want to go home, at any time, just say the word."

I nodded and he helped me up and into the passenger side. My heart was clanging in my ears. I used the short time while he walked around the truck to rub my sweaty palms on my jeans. I was so nervous my teeth were knocking together, but ever so slightly, so maybe he'd never notice. The night had cooled, so it was possible I could pass my chattering teeth off to the weather.

He slid into the drive seat. "Come here." He patted the space on the bench seat beside him. "You cold?"

I scooted over. "A little," I lied.

He started the engine, and turned up the heat.

Then he wrapped an arm around me and pulled me snug against him. "Maybe this will help."

I was going to go up into flames. "What did you want to tell me?"

"We're almost at my house."

I gulped down my nerves, which wasn't easy around the lust lump.

He pulled into the drive of a small house in a residential neighborhood. I glanced around.

"Not where I expected you'd live."

He smiled. "Why's that?"

I shrugged. "No wild parties. No half-naked girls on the lawn."

This time, he laughed. "Sounds like my first couple of years here, but those days are behind me." He opened his door and slid from the truck. He held out his hand to help me exit the same door then locked up the truck and put his arm around my shoulders. "Not that I didn't have fun, because I did, but there came a time when I decided that, if I wanted my NFL dream, I needed to work for it. So, it was out with the parties and in with the studying and workouts."

"You live alone?"

He shook his head. "No. Gunter, our center, lives here too."

I hesitated, pulling him to a stop.

"He isn't here," Zack said. "He leaves every weekend and drives home to see his girlfriend there."

I followed him inside his house to the living room.

"Drink?"

I shook my head.

"I'm going to grab a beer. You sure?"

I shrugged. "I guess you can bring me one too."

I sat on his couch. A moment later, he dropped on the cushion next to me and handed me a beer. Then he put his arm around me and pulled me snugly against him. We both took a sip of beers, then he set his beer on the table, took mine and set it beside his. Then he turned my face toward him. What started as a light kiss quickly evolved into a deeper kiss with tongues twisting together and me sitting in his lap. I sucked on his bottom lip, pulling it into my mouth which elicited a deep groan from him. Our makeup session continued with quickening breaths, hands making tentative touches, and an extremely rigid cock growing under my ass.

"I have a confession," he said against my mouth.

I pulled back. "Oh, yeah? What's that?"

"I've had a thing for you since we met at the freshman orientation."

I frowned. "What? I...I'm sorry. I don't remember that."

With a chuckle, he hugged me tighter. "I see I didn't make the impression on you that you made on me. We had Freshman English together too?"

I knew my eyes were bugging out. "You're kidding me, aren't you?"

"Nope. Some guy swept in on you at that orientation mixer and you stayed with him the rest of the night."

"Ah, Henry."

"Yeah, damn Henry."

I laughed. "We broke up regularly. Why didn't you ask me out?"

He shrugged. "You were my dream girl. You were smart and involved with all kinds of smart people and sorority events, and I was running with a bunch of knuckleheaded jocks. Two different worlds. I kept expecting to forget you."

I smiled. "But you didn't."

He nodded. "I did not forget you. Every time I saw you around campus, you were never alone. You were always with your sisters or some guy."

I arched an eyebrow. "Well, we have some lost time to make up for?"

"Here's the problem." He stroked my cheek. "If this goes to where I'm hoping it will, I'm nervous I'll explode the second I see you naked."

My jaw dropped just a little. I wasn't expecting him to be quite so...honest about where he thought this was going. Not that I had any objections. I'd never felt like this before. Filled with a giddy antic-ipation.

Then Zack took over my mouth, his lips giving me a soft, tender kiss before deepening it. When I gasped, he stroked his tongue inward, toying with mine.

After another breathless kiss, I leaned back. "You're going to explode, huh? Let's see, shall we?" Taking a deep breath for courage, I whipped my shirt over my head and tossed it to the floor. My bra was a simple black lace number that I knew displayed my breasts to their best advantage.

His response was a groan as he quickly began nuzzling his nose along the fleshy swells protruding above my cups. I thrust my breasts upward, seeking...something. He understood my need and dragged down the cups to expose my nipples. His lips latched around one beaded tip and sucked it into his mouth, where the flat of his tongue dragged across the tip.

I squirmed on his lap, pressing against his erection. Moisture oozed from inside of me, and I couldn't help the grinding roll of my hips.

Again, he intuitively recognized my need and quickly thumbed open my pants and slipped his hand inside, his fingers gliding downward until a fingertip found the hard knot at the top of my sex and gave it a gentle rub.

I jerked, giving a soft cry.

His head lifted. His cheeks were reddened, his lips moist and a little swollen. "I don't want this to happen here. I want you in my bed."

I gave him a desperate nod. Anything that he wanted, I'd do if it meant release from this sensual torture.

He slid me off his lap, stood, and captured my hand. Then he dragged me behind him as he moved toward the hallway.

Inside his bedroom, he flicked on a single lamp at his bedside and turned to me. "You sure about this?" he asked.

HOT ASSETS

I gave a quick nod, although my body was suddenly frozen, unmoving. This was really going to happen, and I felt a little overwhelmed.

He knelt and pushed down my pants and my panties, then helped me remove my shoes. When he stood, he reached around my back, unhooked my bra, and dragged it down my arms. When I was naked, he stood back. His gaze swept over me, down then up, then downward again before snagging on my breasts and then my pussy. "Fuck, you're beautiful," he murmured hoarsely.

Gathering my courage, I lifted my chin. "Now, you," I said, proud there wasn't a tremor in my voice. I watched as he stripped, tossing his clothing away and then turning to flip back his covers and sheet.

When he turned away, I couldn't help but admire his lean, muscled frame, his corded thighs, the flexing muscles of his ass. I couldn't wait to touch his perfection, so I didn't, reaching out to stroke my hand over his side and then downward to cup a firm buttock.

He turned quickly and caught my wrist. "Don't. I told you," he said and then turned. My gaze caught on his cock...thick veins riding the shaft, the skin stretched taut around his shaft and gleaming like satin.

"Jesus," he whispered. "Don't even look at it. I won't last, Andi."

I dragged my gaze away, or at least pretended to. From the corner of my eye, I could see his dick pulse.

"Fuck," he said, dragging out the word. "I want this to be good," he muttered. I heard him drag in a sharp breath, then, "Get on the bed," he said. "Lie in the middle on your back. Close your eyes."

I followed his instructions, which he'd delivered in tight, precise syllables. I sensed he was holding onto his control by a thread, and the thought was heady that I could excite him so. When I lay on my back, I placed my hands beside my head and peeked through my slitted eyelids as I watched him tear open a condom packet and then roll the sheath down his length. I envied his hands but noted how quickly he did it like he couldn't bear to touch himself any longer than he had to.

Then he was crawling on the bed, right over me, a knee nudging between both of mine until I opened for him, and then the other entering the space and nudging again until my thighs were spread wide.

"Can I look now?" I whispered.

He shook his head, then said, "No."

"It's not fair, you know."

He bent quickly and engulfed one breast in his mouth, pulling on it, his tongue flicking the tip inside his mouth before he moved across my chest to suck the other into his mouth.

My knees jerked upward, framing his upper thighs. My hips lifted, instinctively seeking his.

When he came off my breast, he rested his forehead against the center of my chest. "Play with your tits, Andi."

I couldn't help it. Surprise had me blinking at him.

"Your tits," he said, his voice deepening. "Touch them."

Then he bent and kissed my sternum before he scooted downward, his gaze locking with mine until I lowered my hands to cup my breasts. His eyes narrowed, and it was like I could hear what he was thinking. He wanted more.

So, I pinched the tips and gave them a little twist, the sting causing my hips to rise again; this time, my mound touched his upper abdomen. My eyelids sank, nearly closing.

He moved downward, kissing and sucking at my skin. His tongue circled my belly button before pressing into it. A quick arc of electricity lifted goose bumps on my skin, and more liquid flowed inside me. When he glided his tongue toward my mound, my breath caught, and I reached out to grip his hair, shocked now that he was going *there*. Yes, I knew it was a thing, but the thought of his face there, smelling me, tasting me—I cringed with embarrassment.

He thumbed my outer labia and lifted his head. "Princess, do you think you won't like it?"

I looked at the ceiling. "I'm afraid *you* won't. That you're only doing this...because...you don't want me to change my mind or because you think I need it."

He stuck out his tongue and licked the tender skin above my mound, all the while staring up at me, waiting for me to lower my gaze. When I did, he said, "Andi. Let go of my hair."

I swallowed hard and nodded, then slowly straightened my fingers.

"Your tits," he said, glancing at my nipples.

"Bossy, aren't you?"

"You'll like this almost as much as I will," he whispered, then dove downward, his tongue lapping through my folds in a long glide, lifting when he touched my swollen clitoris, and damn, now I knew what *that* felt like. I hissed through my teeth, and he chuckled.

"Baby, I've just started."

While I molded my hands over my breasts, his thumbs opened me, and he licked between the inner and outer folds, then nibbled playfully at the edges before he pointed his tongue and circled my opening. He drew back his head and stared downward. "You're not fully...open, baby." His gaze lifted to mine, questioning.

I shrugged. "I've only ever done some heavy petting."

"You've never fucked?"

I grew a little alarmed. His face was still *right there*, and he wanted to have a conversation? Now? "I've never had a man inside me. No."

"But you're beautiful, and I've seen you with that guy..."

"Henry, yeah. But we've never...fucked."

His lips twitched. "Was that hard to say?"

"About as hard as it is to hold a conversation while my pussy is in your face."

He shook his head and then tapped my clitoris. "You sure you want this? With me?"

I couldn't imagine giving my virginity to anyone else. I nodded. "Please."

"Well, this has to go," he said, a finger entering me and rotating. "My dick would shrivel if it ever hurt you."

"No, it wouldn't," I whispered.

"No, it wouldn't," he said softly, "but I'd regret it."

I wrinkled my nose because whatever he was doing was stretching me. Again, he rotated his finger, then thrust another inside, using my moisture to lubricate his fingers as he began stroking into me. Then he bent his head. "Your clit, baby. Ever had a guy suck it?"

"Guys do that?" I said, half-joking because he was already mouthing it, and I was sure my eyes were rolling back into my head as a long, loud moan left my throat.

When he sucked it harder, my hips jerked.

"Too much?" he asked.

"Yeah," I gasped, wondering if it was possible to feel too much pleasure, too much tension.

"You're wet, Andi. So wet," he said, then withdrew his fingers and kissed my clit, my mound, and then moved up my body until his face hovered above mine.

I moved my hands over the crests of his shoulders, down his arms, and over his chest. "Are we going to do it now?"

"What do you want, Andi?"

I gave him a little glare. "You, inside me."

"The words, Andi," he said, one side of his mouth quirking upward.

"Fuck me, Zack. I want your cock."

He laughed. "You're going to have to work on your dirty talk."

"Maybe you could teach me," I said, teasing him. "What should I have said?"

"Oh, the *fuck me* part was pretty good," he said, sliding his hands under my butt while he nudged between my legs, his cock finding my center and then entering me, just the tip.

I made a face.

"That hurt?"

I shook my head. "Just feels...like a lot."

"There's more." He moved deeper inside, just barely, then withdrew until only the tip remained. Then he moved again, going deeper this time.

More moisture filled me, seeping around him, aiding his motions as he began to sink deeper and deeper with each stroke.

"This is fucking incredible. Jesus, Andi," he whispered. "Put your legs around me. Hold onto me."

I wrapped my legs around his hips, which tilted mine, easing his entry. He was moving faster now and so deeply that he rubbed against my clitoris again and again. Tension built inside me, causing my hips to roll and my inner muscles to clasp around him rhythmically. We were both growing slick with exertion; our breaths shortened.

I felt as though something was about to happen, but it was just out of reach. "Zack…"

"I know. Fuck, I know." He shifted, and one hand slid between our bodies. A finger slipped into the top of my folds, gathered moisture, then rubbed against my clit.

It was like he'd pulled a trigger on my desire. I exploded. My back arched, and my fingers dug into his back as pleasure radiated outward from my core. Zack shouted and his movements grew jerky, slowing until he moved in gentle waves against me, more soothing than inflaming. I clutched his back and pressed my face against his hot skin.

His arms came around me, and he rolled us to our sides. "You okay?"

I grinned back at his worried face. "Never better."

He kissed me. "Stay the night?"

I kissed him back and nodded. Now that I'd gotten my V-card notched, I was ready to explore this gift before me. I glanced down between us, then back at Zack, who was now smiling smugly at me. "How long will it take before he's ready again?"

We finally fell asleep around midnight, or at least he did. I couldn't sleep. Emotions were running wild through my system. I'd never felt so much joy and peace as I did beside him in bed. I felt loved and cherished. It didn't take much for me to see us together, a house with two or three children in the yard, and a large golden retriever barking at a squirrel in a tree.

My brain came to a jarring stop.

No. That wasn't my future. I'd spent years dreaming of the day I could take over the family's foundation to use our vast resources to make a difference in people's lives. I couldn't do that with children, a dog, and a husband who was gone all the time playing football.

Zack made me want a future that wasn't what I had planned, and that was dangerous. I'd worked my ass off to get into my dream law school, and here I was seriously giving thought to chunking all that to run away with a guy I'd just slept with.

I slowly turned my head to look at him. God, what a face. What a dream body. He was my fantasy guy come to life, but to have him, I would have to give up law school. My family was counting on me to take the lead at the foundation. We'd talked about it for years. How could I throw all that away for a guy? But, hell, I wanted to. Part of me wanted to implant myself on Zack and never let go. It wasn't possible to connect with someone like I felt I had with Zack. Was it possible to all in love someone in just one night? That kind of stuff only happened in novels and movies. I was much, much too level-headed.

A tear rolled out of the corner of my eye and down the side of my face. I had to let this go. Too many people were counting on me. If I continued to see him...Well, I just couldn't. He made me feel too much. To stay on my life plan, I had to go and never see him again.

More tears joined the first one. My heart split. As

I gently left his bed, I left half of my weeping heart there.

I swept my clothes up and dressed in the living room. I called Brooke and asked her to pick me up. Like a good sister, she did and asked no questions. She hugged me and let me cry all the way home.

I told both of my sisters they were not to put a call from Zack through to me, and to tell him I'd gotten back with Henry. If I heard Zack's voice, I knew I could never stay away. So, it was better not to take his calls, as much as it pained me.

It was so hard to stay away from him. For the entire hellish semester, I went to class and I came home. I never went back to the Orange Cactus. As soon as I took my last exam, I left town as fast as possible. If I said I never thought of him again, that'd be total bullshit.

He lived on in my dreams, and I'd supposed, he always would.

Four

*C*urrent Day

"How have you been, Andi?" Zack asked.

I shrugged, but my heart ran track around my chest. "Good. Busy. You?"

"Good. Busy." He gave me that oh-so-dangerous smile. "It's late. We can play catch up another time."

"Sure," I said, relieved he was letting the subject of our time together go...at least for now. I don't think I could handle that discussion tonight. I glanced over to Baxter. I might have frowned.

"What's wrong?" he asked. "Is taking care of Baxter a problem?"

I wrinkled my nose. "Not really, but I've never had responsibility for a dog. I'm not exactly sure what I need to do or not do."

"Dogs like Baxter are easy. Soft bed. Food. Fresh water. And maybe a new chew toy now and then."

"You sound like you know all about dogs. Do you have one?"

"Not right now. I'm working all kinds of crazy hours, and it wouldn't be fair to a dog to be left alone that much."

I blew out a long breath. "I know I had no choice, but I work long hours too. What am I going to do with him while I'm gone?"

"Take him with you," he said with a shrug. "You're the boss, right? Who's going to complain? Plus, he's tiny. Nobody may even notice."

I was surprised he was aware of my work. Had he followed my career the way I'd followed his while he's been with the Philadelphia Eagles? Or had he maybe gotten one of the foundation's renovation grants and that's how he knew?

"I am the boss," I confirmed, "but taking a dog to the office? My staff will think I've lost my mind." I sighed. "A problem to solve later. Maybe I will. Can you help me load up what I'll need to take to my house for Baxter?"

Thirty minutes later, Zack was loaded down like Baxter's personal pack mule. He had Baxter's bed, a bag of dog toys, and a sack of premium dog food. I had clipped Baxter onto a lead and carried his empty food and water bowls. I set Lillian's house alarm and locked the front door.

"I'm glad you had a key," he said as we walked across the lawn to my house. "I wondered how I'd lock that old door when we left."

"Which reminds me...Why did you come over anyway? I mean, surely checking on your neighbors in the middle of the night isn't your standard nightly routine."

"You left the front door standing wide open."

I groaned. "I was afraid of that." I glanced over and got a jolt of electricity to my heart. I needed to keep my eyes straight ahead. "I was in such a hurry." I chuckled. "You know, I was sure you were there to mug us...or worse."

He stopped walking and stared at me. I stopped and stared back.

"Do I look like a criminal to you?"

I shrugged. "Not to offend, but with that scruff and your long hair, you do look kind of rough."

To my surprise, he grinned. "Thanks. I'm supposed to."

"Hmm."

We climbed the stairs to my porch. "Come on in and leave that stuff anywhere."

He followed me inside, then glanced around and whistled. "Totally renovated?"

"Yes."

"Plumbing and wiring?"

I nodded. "Since I wanted to live here, I needed to feel safe. It's pretty much been complete rebuild from top to bottom. The wiring was old knob and tubing so I knew it had to go. I didn't want to worry about electrical fires. Plus, this was my great-grandparents' place and I knew I had to do it right. Lillian mentioned you were in the old Skaggs place. How far along are you with reno-vations?"

"Just started, actually. Seems like every time I turn around, I find a new problem."

"That's how it is with these old houses. I'd offer you a tour, but..." I shrugged.

Zack stepped back. "Say no more. It's late. I'll drop Baxter's things over there and get gone."

He set the bed, food, and bowls near the entrance to my formal living room and turned back toward the front door.

"Well, good night," I said. "Thanks again for helping with Baxter's move."

Damn him. He smiled and brushed a wavy lock off his forehead. I felt a strong tug in my gut right behind my belly button. It took my breath away while waking up my lady parts that'd been dormant longer than I wanted to admit.

"You'll do great with Baxter. Good night." He turned the knob to open the door and looked back. "You look great, Andi. It was so good to see you again. Tell your sisters hello from me."

As soon as he was gone, I locked up and reset the house alarm, all the while carrying Baxter in my left arm, which was beginning to ache from his eight-pound body.

"Okay, buddy. Let's get you settled," I said, putting him on his four legs. "No time like the present to get you settled.

I gathered up his bed and bowls and headed for the kitchen, assuming that making a place for him there made the most logical sense. I decided the perfect space for his meal area, then filled one bowl

49

with fresh water and the other with dry kibble. Then I placed the dog bed near both.

"Okay then. This looks perfect, right?"

Baxter tilted his head as though thinking about my comment.

"Night, boy. See you in the morning." I flipped off the light to head back to my bed.

A soft whimper stopped me dead in my tracks. I flipped the light back on. The poor dog hadn't moved an inch. When I flipped the light off again, another heartbreaking cry of distress grabbed and squeezed my heart. I turned on the lights. Lillian never went anywhere without him, so he probably wasn't used to being left alone in the kitchen.

With a resigned sigh, I hefted him back into my arms, tucked his bed under my arm, and headed to my bedroom.

"Just tonight," I told him.

His answer was a long lick to my nose. I shook my head with a laugh.

In my room, I set his bed on the floor and Baxter on the soft cushion. Then I collapsed back into my sheets. As soon as I turned my bedside lamp off, darkness swamped every corner of the room. I heard a quiet plop on my mattress, followed by a slight movement. A tiny warm body curled into the small of my back, and Baxter let out a long sigh.

"Fine," I muttered. "It's only for tonight because I know you're upset about Lillian."

Baxter shifted up the bed and laid his head next to mine with another sigh.

Most mornings, I was up and in the shower by five-thirty. As Baxter and I had finally gotten to bed at close to four, I still had ninety minutes to nap.

Sleep didn't want to come. I stared at the ceiling, my last semester at the University of Texas scrolling through my brain like a movie. That single night with Zack as vivid and real as though no time had passed.

Dallas was a huge city. Texas was an enormous state. The last time I'd known Zack's whereabouts had been when he was in Philadelphia. I'd lost track when he'd left the team. I'd had no idea he was in Dallas. What were the odds that my once-in-a-life-time fling, which had occurred two hundred miles and thirteen years ago would end up living across the street? And that he'd be a cop. I tried not to let myself relive that time with him very often. Those memories hurt. I know why I'd done what I had, but that didn't make the memories easier. It'd been clear to me that I was facing a fork in my life. One way led to where I was today. The other? Who knows what that life would have been?

What a chickenshit I'd been. Sneaking out of his house and then not taking his calls. I'd even gotten Claudia to tell him I'd gotten back with Henry, which would never have happened. It'd taken a while, but we'd both moved on. For him, it'd been the NFL draft and a life in the pros. For me, it'd been four more years of school at Yale Law.

When my alarm rang, I groaned. I was exhausted. As Zack had pointed out last night, I was the boss. I could call in. I could work from home. My assistant could forward anything I'd need.

However, again as he'd said, I was the boss, and as such, it was my responsibility to set a good work ethic for the staff. Other than Robin, my assistant, I was usually the first in and last out. How could I expect my staff to work hard if I didn't?

A tiny, pink tongue flicked my cheek. I couldn't hold back the smile. I turned my head and looked at my tiny houseguest. "You know, I brought your bed up here so you could sleep in it."

His tongue curled out of his mouth as he yawned.

"Yeah, that's what I thought. That dog bed is all for show. Well, come on. Let's get up and get moving. I guess you get to learn how to run the Carmichael Foundation today."

Since I knew I'd be late to the office, I didn't have time to make a stop to get what Baxter would need. I certainly wasn't going to haul his bed and bowls back and forth every day. My assistant, Robin, was great with strange requests. Her response to today's texts should be interesting.

Me: I need a couple of items for my office. Can you grab them on your way in?

Robin: Sure. No problem. What do you need?

Me: Quality dog food, water and
food bowls, and a comfortable, but
smallish, dog bed.

Robin: ....

I grinned as I watched the dots on Robin's reply appear and disappear. I'd bet money she was writing and deleting messages not quite sure what to say.

Robin: Okay. You got me. In all the years I've worked for you, you've rarely left me speechless, but congratulations, I am speechless. You got a dog? Since yesterday?

Me: Temporarily. I swear. Long story, but my neighbor had to go to the hospital last night and I have her dog.

Robin: Ah. Big dog?

Me: He thinks so, but only about eight pounds.

Robin: Got it. See you in the office.

And this was why Robin was an excellent assistant. She'd been thrown a little by my request, but was still ready to grab the reins and do what needed to be done.

At seven, I walked Baxter outside to do his business before calling the hospital to check on Lillian. Since I'm not her family—I should have lied and said I was Lillian's daughter—there wasn't much information forthcoming. I'd make time today to get away from the office to go by the hospital and check on Lilliam myself.

Once Baxter was finished watering about ten different spots in my yard, I loaded him into my car and headed to the office. If he was with me very long and kept going to the office, I might to look into a doggie seat for him.

"Well, today should be interesting," I told him.

His reply was a yip and lick to my nose.

I assumed he agreed.

Five

I n my life, I've had MY fair share of the spotlight. However, I've never paraded naked into a room, but the way heads wheeled around to watch me walk in with Baxter, I can only assume it would feel something like this. I'd sort of thought everyone might glance at our entrance and then return to their work. Yeah, no. Baxter, in all his handsomeness, pulled the staff from their offices and cubicles to pet, kiss, nuzzle, and basically love on Baxter like he was a rock star. He took it all in stride as his due.

It took a while before I could separate my staff from Baxter and all the doting. When I finally reach my office, Robin stood in the doorway watching our approach. As we neared, she crouched down and held out a doggie treat. Baxter sniffed, and using all eight of his pounds, pulled me toward Robin and her bribe.

"Dog treats?" I asked with a side-eye. "I don't remember ordering those."

Robin grinned up at me from where she was rubbing all over Baxter's quivering body. "I love dogs. We always had three or four in the house when I was growing up."

"How did I not know that?"

Robin kissed the top of Baxter's head and stood. "The subject never came up."

"You have a dog now?"

Robin shook her head. "Not right now. My last boyfriend hated animals in the house, so I couldn't get one."

"Didn't you dump that guy?"

"Yep. Last month." Robin reached down and picked up Baxter. "Now that you mention it, I think I'll start looking for a dog that needs a good home." Baxter licked her nose, and she laughed. "And what's his—or is it her?—name?"

"This is Baxter. He's Lillian's dog. The last thing she made me swear before she left for the hospital was that I would take Baxter until she comes home."

"Poor Lillian. How is she this morning?"

"I called, but the hospital wouldn't give me any information since I'm not family. I thought I'd go up there at lunch, if you don't mind keeping Baxter."

Robin's face lit up. "I'd love to."

"Let's take a look at my schedule and see what I can reschedule for today."

Carrying the tiny dog in the crock of her arm, Robin jostled her mouse on her desk to wake up her computer and opened the calendar. "Looks pretty clear. You'd set aside most of this week to work on your report to the foundation board. However, you do have lunch scheduled with Richard today."

Richard Pittman was an investment banker I'd been seeing off and on for a few months. He was charming, polite, well-dressed, and attentive, both in bed and out. However, he'd never set my heart racing nor my belly squeezing when we were together. I'd hoped, with time, he would grow on me, but he hadn't, and lately, I'd given thought to ending the relationship.

"Cancel lunch with Richard. Tell him something came up. He'll understand."

Robin nodded. "Sure. Are you in or out to staff today?"

On days before my meeting with the foundation board, which was comprised of my sisters, our parents, our grandparents, and two non-voting advisors, I usually spent hours preparing my presentation, reports, and graphs while trying to anticipate their questions. These meetings were primarily a way to keep the family informed of foundation business. Rarely was there much disagreement with the foundation's direction. My pet project was Carmichael Gardens, so I always felt a little pressure to present that project in the most favorable light. So far, all the grants and renovations were on track.

"I'm in to staff if you can't handle whatever the issue is. I want to look over all the grants for Carmichael Gardens today. Can you get those together for me?"

"Of course." Robin thrust Baxter toward Andi.

"I'll call your lunch date first and then get the grant information to you."

Baxter settled into my arms. "Perfect. Oh, and can you call the hospital and check on Lillian Branson? Pretend you're her granddaughter or something. I want to go up at lunch and see her if I can."

"I've got it."

Over the next couple of hours, I worked undisturbed except for a text message from Richard expressing—in ever so polite terms—his disappointment in not seeing me for lunch and asking me to meet him for dinner. Not nice of me, but I used Baxter as my excuse for declining dinner. As I did, I realized again that the time had come to nip this dead flower off the limb. As much as I would love to send a breakup text, my mom would have kittens. I could hear Mom now, "Very crass. Beneath you, Andrea. Face your actions head-on."

Fine, but not tonight.

I tried to work. I stared at the words and figures on the sheets of paper, but my mind drifted to last night, specifically to Zack Noles. I'd always thought he'd had an interesting face, and adulthood hadn't changed my opinion. Even through his scruff, I could see he was still incredibly handsome. With its creases, stubble, and occasional scars, his face told an interesting story of his life. Definitely something any woman would want to study in minute detail. He was still broad-shouldered with muscular arms, and narrow hips. He wore his confidence like a comfortable shirt. I wondered where he wore his gun because I sure hadn't seen one on him last night.

Since work couldn't hold my attention, I might as well check in with my sister and see what was happening with her day.

Claudia, aka Dee, Carmichael answered with, "No, you cannot borrow my pink silk dress, or any of my clothes, now that I think about it."

I laughed. I'd borrowed Dee's favorite dress when we'd been in high school and had gotten thrown into a swimming pool as a prank. The dress had been a pale pink silk and had been completely destroyed. My sister had never let me live that down.

"Well," I said with an exaggerated huff. "That's some way to treat your older, wiser sister."

"Older by thirty minutes, I'll grant you that. Wiser? Let me see your LSAT scores again."

I laughed again. We'd spent our entire lives together, so when it had come to law school, we'd gone different ways. I'd headed to Yale, while Dee had gone the Harvard route. Even from a distance and being in different schools, our competitive streak had continued. I doubted that would change any time soon.

"So, what's up?" Dee asked.

"Can't I just call my sister because I missed her?"

"You can, but you don't. Besides, I'll see you in a few days at the foundation meeting and you only call when you need something."

I winced. "I should probably be insulted, but

sadly, you're right. I promise to do better in the future."

"Okay," her sister replied, "but today's call is about...?"

Sighing, I asked, "Do you remember a Zack Noles from college?"

Dee laughed. "Are you crazy? Everyone knew Zack Noles. BMOC. Handsome as sin. A tight ass that made every college girl stare. Seemed like every female tried to get his attention. You got his attention and passed. I never understood that. Anyway, why?"

"I ran into him last night."

"Oh, yeah? How does he look? Still sex-on-a-stick body?"

I swallowed hard. "He looks pretty good."

"So, tell me about your reunion. Did you bring up that night in college?"

"Of course not. I, um..." I winced. "I pretended that I could barely remember that night."

Dee howled. "I swear, Andi. You kill me. What happened?"

"You remember my neighbor, Lillian?"

"Of course. Nice lady."

"She fell, maybe broke her hip or leg, I'm not sure. She called me to come over at two this morning. While I was there waiting on the ambulance, Zack came in to see why her front door was open,"

"Wait. How does Zack know Lillian?"

"Here's an interesting tidbit. Zack lives in the house across the street that's undergoing renovation."

"*Really*?" Dee drew out the word. "And you didn't know?"

"I didn't know."

"Back to my question, why was he checking on Lillian in the middle of the night?"

"I didn't get a chance to say, but he's a detective with the Dallas PD. He was just getting home and saw the door open."

"Ohhh, a personal security guard. Nice."

"You think you're so funny."

"I know, right?" Dee chuckled. "But back to Lillian...How is she doing today?"

"Robin called the hospital, claiming to be Lillian's granddaughter. All she got was Lillian was in surgery."

"Yikes. That doesn't sound good at all."

"No, it doesn't. I plan to head up there shortly and find out what I can."

"Well, this puts me in an awkward spot."

"How? Oh, hold on a sec. Robin is waving from my door." I covered the receiver with my hand. "What?"

"Detective Noles is here to see you." Robin pumped her eyebrows and mouthed, "Yummy."

"Dee, I'll need to call you back. Zack Noles is here —no wait, he just walked into my office uninvited."

I pointed to the phone as if Zack was too dense to understand I was talking on it. Why was I getting so flustered? Stress sweat trickled down my back. My heart began pounding like a base drum. What was wrong with me? Zack was simply standing in my office, not removing his clothes…not that a man removing his clothes in my office was something that'd ever happened. Still, it could happen, right?

Baxter's head lifted off my lap to check out all the commotion. As soon as Baxter saw Zack, his tail began to wag—Baxter's tail, that was. He jumped down and ran across the room. Zack leaned over, scratched the dog's back, and then picked him up.

Sadly, I could understand Baxter's enthusiasm. Who wouldn't like a good *back scratch* from the sexy cop?

I cleared my throat. "I'll call you back." I could still hear Dee talking when I hung up.

"Detective," I said, not happy with my breathy tone. I cleared my throat. "To what do I owe the pleasure?"

"Thought I'd check on Lillian before I headed into the station and wondered if you'd like to go with me and, maybe, grab some lunch while we're out."

"I would. Hold on. Robin."

"Right here," my assistant answered from the doorway.

"I'm going to the hospital with Detective Noles. Can you keep an eye on Baxter?"

"Sure. Come on, big guy. It's you and me for lunch." She fluttered her fingers at Zack.

"Oh," he said. "You mean the dog." He grinned as he passed Baxter over. "When you said big guy, well…"

Robin chuckled and took Baxter. "You two have a nice visit."

"Feel free to use my office since all of Baxter's things are in here."

"I planned ahead," Robin said. "Don't worry about us. Isn't that right, Baxter?" She finished her question with her nose nuzzled into Baxter's soft hair.

"Call me if you need me," I said.

As we walked toward the elevator, my stomach quivered with nerves. First because I was afraid he would bring up that night we'd had, and I had no explanation for my actions. Well, I had an explanation. I just didn't want to tell him. And second, I was walking with Zack Noles. Just being in his presence again set off ridiculous waves of lust.

I might be risking my heart being around him again.

"Nice offices," Zack said.

"Thanks. My staff works hard, and I want them comfortable in their jobs." The elevator doors opened, and we stepped in. "Plus, I like to retain staff. I figured out a long time ago that it's costly to the business side to have lots of staff turnover."

He nodded. "If only the DPD thought the same way," he said with a grin that did all kinds of things to my belly.

On the first floor, he directed me to a sedan that did everything but scream "Cop car."

I lifted a brow. "You're parked in the fire lane."

His grin grew wider. "One of the perks of my job." He opened the passenger door. "I didn't figure I would be gone long."

I slipped onto the seat, and he closed the door. I noticed the official *On Duty* placard on the dash. When he got behind the steering wheel, I pointed to the placard. "That's handy. Can I get one, too?"

"Absolutely. Finish the police academy, put your time in on the streets, pass the detective exam, and get a promotion. Then, it's all yours."

I chuckled. "Thanks, but I'll just pay for parking."

When we got to the hospital, he pulled into a spot in front of the hospital and parked. He flipped the police placard on the dash.

I rolled my eyes. "Man, I have *got* to figure out how to snag one of those."

"I'll be keeping a close eye on mine."

I laughed.

We were directed to the second floor by the lobby receptionist. Lillian's room was near the nurses' station, a prime location should anything go wrong.

The head of the hospital bed was raised slightly. The over-the-bed rolling table held a congealed breakfast that'd barely been touched. Lillian was out cold, her mouth slightly open, a soft snore filling the room. Both legs were extended, each with a pressure cuff inflating and deflating on a schedule.

"I hate to wake her up," I whispered.

His answer was a nod.

"Her color looks better," I said. "Not so pale."

The door opened and a woman hurried in. Her blue scrubs were covered with a white lab coat with

SUZY HELMS, RN embroidered on the shoulder. Her official hospital ID badge hung around her neck.

"Good morning," she chirped brightly. "Are you family?"

"Neighbors," I said.

"Very close neighbors," Zack said. "We are the ones who were with her last night. How's she doing?" He flipped open his badge.

"She's doing well."

"She's not in much pain, is she?" I asked, my brow furrowed with worry.

The nurse checked the IV and entered something into the room computer. "We're keeping her comfortable."

"Will she need to go to rehab?" I asked.

"These types of injuries usually do. I'm just her nurse today, not her case coordinator, but given her age and the break in her leg, my money is on probably so."

I took Lillian's hand into mine. It was warm and dry, but Lillian didn't respond to the touch. "Has anyone else been to see her?" she asked.

"Not while I've been on today."

Zack's phone rang. He left the room while pulling it from his pocket.

"Thank you for taking such good care of her. She's a special person."

The nurse gave me a kind smile. "I can see that. Let me know if she wakes up."

Zack was coming back in as the nurse left.

"We need to go," he said, his tone brusque and short.

I looked at the serious expression on his face and nodded. "Okay." I squeezed Lillian's hand. "I'll be back," I whispered.

"Mind the stairs?" Zack asked as he headed to the closest exit.

"No, but what's happening?"

"The alarm is going off at Lillian's house."

I hurried down the stairs with him, glad I hadn't worn high heels. As we reached the street, I was also thankful for the placard I'd made fun of. Now I saw he really did need to get to his car as quickly as possible when he got a call. It made sense that he wouldn't want to be parked high in a garage that required an elevator and a long walk to reach his car. Precious minutes would've been lost. Maybe not key for this situation, but certainly in other cases.

"I've got my door," I said, grabbing the handle. "Let's get moving."

He gave me a curt nod as we both slid into our seats. "Buckle up," he said, flipping on a loud siren.

I did and was glad I had when he wheeled from his parking place at full speed. I hadn't realized I was a speed junkie until the traffic parted and we flew down streets toward our neighborhood.

"You're grinning, Princess. Like driving fast, do you?"

"Don't misunderstand. I'm worried about Lillian's house, but there's something about racing through the street that's exhilarating."

He glanced over at me with a grin and then turned his attention back to driving. "I have a feeling I'm going to be fixing some speeding tickets for you in the future."

I held on as he took a sharp corner.

On a good day, our neighborhood was a good forty-five-minute drive from this hospital. Today, traffic parted like the Red Sea for Moses. A short twenty minutes later, he turned onto our street. Two Dallas police cars were parked in front of Lillian's house, their lights flashing. Zack parked next to the patrol cars.

"Wait here," he said.

I opened her door and stepped out. "Yeah, no."

He rolled his eyes.

"I don't take orders well," I said, walking beside him to the officer on the sidewalk.

"I'll remember that." Zack showed his badge to the patrol office. "Detective Noles. What's going on?"

"The call came in about thirty minutes ago. We checked around the house. Rear door was open. No windows broken. Front door is how we found it."

All heads turned toward the house. The front door was shut.

"Is it locked?" I asked.

"Yes, ma'am," the fresh-faced officer said.

Ma'am? I suddenly felt much older than thirty-six.

"Have you cleared the house?' Zack asked.

"Yes. No one's in there."

"Wait here," Zack said to me. He squinted his

eyes. "I mean it this time. Wait here until I make sure it's safe." He looked at the two officers who joined them. "Someone stay here and make sure she doesn't move. I want to check out the house myself before I let her go in."

I huffed. "God. So bossy."

"Let's go."

Two officers went with him while a third stayed with me.

"So, what's your name?" I asked.

"Paul Rowe, ma'am."

"You don't have to 'ma'am' me."

"Yes, ma'am."

I gave up. "Did you go inside?"

"I did."

"Is everything messed up in there?" I winced thinking of all the possible damage that could have happened. Lillian had some beautiful and expensive antiques, not to mention all the sterling silver pieces. I had no idea if Lillian kept any cash around or even if she had a safe.

"Not too bad," the patrolman said, interrupting my thoughts. "Only a couple of rooms look disturbed. Looks like maybe an office and a bedroom."

"How'd he get in?"

Before he answered, Zack whistled from the front door. "It's safe. Come on up."

I hurried up the walk, my low heels clicking on the concrete sidewalk. "The patrolman said two rooms were messed up…?"

"Only two were obviously disturbed. I want you to take a look and see if you can tell if anything is missing, especially from her office."

I frowned and winced. "I'll look, but honestly, I don't know that I've even been in her office. I mean, I've never had a reason to go in there. But I'll take a look."

I gasped when I walked into the office. Drawers had been left hanging open. Papers had been flung all over the floor. The cushions from the couch were standing on end. A desk lamp was lying on its side on the floor, the crystal lampshade shattered, the individual shards shining as Zack's flashlight passed over them. A black safe sat in a closet, its door hanging open.

"How did they get into the safe?" I asked.

Zack pointed to an index card on the rug. "Combination. Whoever was here may have torn this place apart looking for that. Or maybe they were looking for something else. Can you see if anything is missing?"

I shook her head. "Honestly, I have no clue."

"Follow me through the house. Tell me if you see anything amiss."

When we reached the living room, I pointed to an empty shelf. "There were some vases and small *objets d'art* there. Lillian and her husband picked them up on their trip to China and Southeast Asia maybe ten years ago."

"Can you describe them?"

"I can do better. There was an article in Dallas

Living magazine maybe three years ago. That's how I met Lillian. There were pictures of those pieces." I looked at Zack. "They were quite valuable, both in memories for her and in monetary value."

He nodded. "Anything else?"

"Not that I can see. Have you checked her silver closet?"

Zack looked over at the responding officer and arched a brow.

"I didn't see a silver closet," the patrolman said.

Internally, I groaned. That didn't sound good. "This way," I said, mentally crossing my fingers that the intruder hadn't known about Lillian's hidden closet.

The cops followed me into the kitchen. The sink of dirty dishes remained, reminding me that Lillian had lied to us last night. I'd been pretty sure at the time, and now with the missing art pieces Lillian and her husband had collected during their journeys, combined with the open safe, I was positive. I just didn't understand why she'd lie.

In the kitchen, I went to the pantry and pressed on a wall. There was a click, and the wall opened into a small interior closet.

"We didn't see this," the patrolman confessed. "Good hiding spot."

Zack flashed his light over the empty shelves. "It's a burglary. Call it in."

"I'm sick for Lillian. I'm glad she wasn't here, but this is going to break her heart," I said as Zack and I walked slowly back to his car. "Wait." I stopped and grabbed his arm. "The alarm went off when they left, right?"

Zack nodded.

"So how did they get in?" I asked.

He gave me a sideways look and lifted an eyebrow. "You tell me."

We took a few more steps, my brain whirling like a computer. I stopped and grabbed his arm again. "He was already in the house. Crappola. He was in the house when I locked up." I squeezed Zack's arm. "He was in the house while we were downstairs with Lillian. She lied to us."

"I know."

"When did you know?"

"Last night. Are you just discovering that?"

I blew out a sigh. "No. I knew she lied last night. The dishes?"

He nodded.

"So, what was all that nonsense about the stepstool?"

"I wanted Lillian to think I believed her. I didn't know why she wasn't telling us the truth." He shrugged. "I thought maybe she'd had dinner with a gentleman and was embarrassed to say."

"Then this person, whoever he was, had all night to search her house and stack up what he wanted to take. Probably didn't take long to toss things into a car."

"Especially if he had a helper."

I nodded with a frown. "On the outside, waiting."

"Exactly."

We reached his car and he opened my door. "I might make a detective out of you yet," he said, tapping the end of my nose.

That simple touch sent tiny electrical volts through my body. And, as much as I disliked my body's betrayal, it also sent a shiver down my spine.

He drove me back to my office, neither of us speaking much. I was thinking about who might have been in the house. I had no idea what Zack was thinking. After a quick glance over at his stoic face, I decided he would be killer at poker.

When he pulled into the circle drive in front of my building, I said, "Thanks. I'm glad I got to see Lillian. Don't bother walking me up. I'm good."

Before I could make my escape, he wrapped his fingers around my wrist. I turned back, my forehead furrowed. "Did I forget something?" I asked

"One day in the very near future, we will talk about that night. I will want to know why you left like you did."

Six

My heart was still racing as I stepped off the elevator. Was his statement a warning? A threat? And what was there to say about the way I'd snuck off like a thief in the night? It had happened. It was in the past. What else was there? We'd been young and foolish.

Before I could expend too much mental exertion on that question, another came into view. What was going on in my office?

As I neared, I couldn't stop the wide grin that spread across my face. A sheet of paper had been taped over my nameplate, Andrea Carmichael, CEO. The paper now identified my office as, "Baxter's Play Pen. Hours by Appointment Only."

From my office, the sounds of female voices and giggles echoed into the hall. Since we were the only inhabitants of this level, the noise wouldn't bother any of the businesses on the lower floors, but I did wonder what was going on.

When the office had been constructed, the primary office—mine—had had an outer office—Robin's—designed for the CEO's assistant. There was a door between our offices and a door that led from Robin's office to the hall. The outer door to Robin's office was open. Chairs dragged from other staff offices filled Robin's area. A baby gate had been set up across the door.

I stepped up to the door and stopped by the gate. "Well, looks like I missed a party."

Robin looked up with a grin. "Not my fault. I swear." She raised her hand as though swearing-in for legal testimony. "Baxter sent out a companywide email inviting everyone to drop by to meet him." She shrugged. "What could I do?"

I chuckled. "What indeed? Where is the little troublemaker?"

"Over here," Miranda from accounting said.

I looked over and shook my head. Baxter was stretched across her lap, four legs in the air while Miranda rubbed his belly. "Lord. Lillian will have her hands full with him when you ladies get done."

I moved the gate and stepped into the office. At my entrance, ten women stood, collected their lunch debris, and began rolling their chairs back to their offices. Miranda passed Baxter back into Robin's outstretched hands.

"Don't leave on my account," I said to the group.

"They aren't. We were getting ready to break up before you got here."

"I'll be back at two for Baxter," Karen from legal

said. She nuzzled Baxter's nose. "See you then, honey."

I looked at Robin with a questioning expression.

"Oh, they all volunteered to help walk Baxter while he's here." She pointed to a piece of notebook paper on her desk with names and times written in ink and then shrugged. "They made a schedule so everyone gets a turn taking him outside."

"They don't have to do that," I protested. "I didn't bring him here to make more work for everyone." I felt guilty that I was imposing on my staff like that.

My assistant laughed. "I had to draw the line at sharing him in their offices—so, no. He isn't a problem, are you, honey?" Baxter licked her nose. "He agrees. He's no problem and insists on coming to work with you every day."

I sighed. "Order a doggie booster seat for my car, will you?"

"Yes!" Robin said. "You're a regular working guy now. I'll figure out how to get you on the payroll." She set the dog on the floor, and she and Baxter followed me into the main office. "You did have some calls while you were out." Robin frowned "You were gone a lot longer than I thought you would be."

"I know," I said as I replaced my purse in a drawer and then sat in my chair. "We saw Lillian. She was pretty much out of it. Then, before we could get lunch, Zack got a call that Lillian's house alarm was going off, so we headed over there."

Robin took a seat in front of my desk. "Oh, no. How bad?"

I lifted Baxter into my lap. "Looks like whoever it was got some valuable art pieces and all of her sterling silver."

"Jewelry?"

I shrugged. "I honestly don't know, and we may not know until Lillian is more alert." I gritted my teeth in anger. "But this makes me so mad." My harsh tone upset Baxter. He nuzzled under my chin as though trying to calm me. I nuzzled the top of his head and stroked a hand down his soft back. "Thanks. I needed that."

"Well, I hate hearing about that." Robin laid a stack of phone messages on the desk. "The only one that seemed urgent was from your sister, Dee. She said to have you call her as soon as you get in. She tried your cell, but it went to voice mail."

"I'll call her now."

Robin stood to leave but stopped. "I've enjoyed having Baxter around today. I think everyone else did, also. He hasn't been a problem at all, and you know I'd tell you if he was. I hope you'll continue to bring him in with you." She shut the door as she left my office.

"Hear that?" I whispered to Baxter. "You're a hit."

Baxter licked my nose as if to say, "I know."

My sister, Dee, answered on the first ring. "We need to talk."

I frowned at my sister's tone. "Okay, sure. What's up?"

"Not on the phone. I have a client sitting in my waiting room, and I need some time and your attention to go over some legal papers with you."

"Sure. Come by tonight if you want."

"I'll be by about six, okay?"

"Sure. What's this about?"

"Lillian Branson."

"Ah. Okay. See you then."

Hmm, very interesting. Since Dee did a lot of trust and estate law, I supposed that was what this was all about. But, still...what did Lillian's legal affairs have to do with me?

There was a knock a second before Robin opened her door. "I grabbed you a sandwich since you missed lunch."

There was a reason I overpaid my assistant. Replacing her would be impossible.

Baxter and I arrived home in time for me to change clothes and set up a cheese and cracker tray to go with a bottle of merlot. I added two wine glasses to the tray and carried all of it onto the deck overlooking my backyard. I poured a glass of wine for myself and settled onto a lounger. As I sipped wine, I watched Baxter sniff and inspect every blade of grass. It took a while, but he finally found the perfect spot to do his afternoon business. I saluted him with my wine glass.

As I waited for Dee, my thoughts naturally went to Zack. His comment about that night rang in my ears. I'd been at the Orange Cactus with my sisters when he'd come in, but I'd been on beer number one. I'd been in complete control of all my actions. As soon as he'd slipped up next to me, and whispered, "Hello, Princess. I've been looking for you," all the control over my feelings and emotions had evaporated like dry ice. Hell, he'd pulled me toward him like a magnet to metal.

Baxter's excited yip brought me out of my deep memories. I turned toward the gate in time to see it swing open and Dee stride in—and really, stride was the perfect verb for her. She'd always had that strong, assertive air around her. During law school, she'd added the art of intimidating her opponent with her approach technique. Her head was held high. Her gaze was fixed directly ahead. Each step was confident, each foot placed firmly in place before the next step. The whole walk happened in such a fast and self-assured poise that the affected person felt the intimidation but could rarely determine what caused it.

"Don't try your lawyer strut on me," I called. "It doesn't work."

Dee laughed. "Sadly, I think this is my normal walk now. Maybe it's the reason no guy ever asks me out."

"You just haven't found anyone good enough for you."

"Maybe." Dee knelt to greet Baxter, who'd run from the far end of the yard. "Hello, precious," she said, picking him up. Baxter snuggled against her chest.

"You want a dog?" I asked with a grin.

"Not right now, but if I got one, I'd want it to be just like Baxter."

"He is a good boy," I agreed. "You seem like you know him."

"We've met," Dee replied before dropping into the lounge chair next to me.

"Wine?"

"Is that whine with an h or wine without?"

"Wine, without an h, but feel free to unload on me if you need an ear." I poured a second glass of wine and passed it to her. "Cheers."

Dee lifted her glass in an air salute and then took a long gulp.

"Thirsty much?" I asked with a questioning lift of my eyebrow.

"High alcohol tolerance," Dee said.

"Those good old college years finally paying off." She laughed.

"Seriously, Dee, why so stressed out?"

Dee sighed and refilled her glass. "I'm worried about your neighbor."

"Lillian or Zack?"

Dee lifted her glass in a mocking salute. "Excellent question. I was thinking of Lillian, but if you want to talk about Zack first, I'm all ears."

I smiled. "We'll stick with Lillian for now. What's up?"

"Right." Dee set her glass on the side table and

lifted her enormous leather tote bag onto the chair. "Did you know Lillian was one of my clients?"

I thought about her question as I watched Baxter roll and chase an inflatable ball around in the grass. "I guess I'm not all that surprised. You do have a reputation for dealing with large estates and foundations. When did Lillian come to you?"

"About eighteen months ago or so. She wanted to set up a trust and make sure if anything happened to her that Baxter would be taken care of."

"She does love that dog."

We both watched him play.

"It's hard not to get attached to him," I said. "He a charmer.

"Lillian agrees." Dee pulled a three-ring notebook from her bag. "One of her requests was to have you read these papers when I thought the time was right. Since she's been healthy and active, and has continued to travel often, I never felt the time was right. But after last night, I think it's time." She held up the binder. "This is her medical power of attorney and her financial power of attorney should she become incapacitated. Those are the two things I want you to read. The rest of the paperwork details her trust and the distribution of her funds at her death."

I took the notebook and flipped to the tab for Medical Power of Attorney, followed by the tab labeled Financial Power of Attorney. I was surprised Lillian had added me to both of these since we'd only known each other for about three years. But we'd become very close. Still, it was sobering to realize how alone Lillian was in the world with only a grandson, and nobody knew where he was. As an attorney myself, I took this responsibility seriously.

"Have you notified the hospital about the medical POA?" I asked.

Dee nodded. "I faxed that over as soon as I heard about Lillian."

"And you didn't think I needed to know this before now?"

"You did, yes, but Lillian didn't want you burdened with extra responsibilities unless it became unavoidable. That woman has an independent streak a mile wide. I did speak with Brooke and asked her to check on Lillian. While she couldn't go into the specifics because of HIPPA laws and patient confidentiality, she did say that, in her medical opinion, Lillian's treatment thus far has been exactly what she would've recommended, so there have been no medical situations that would require your attention."

"What about her Medicare coverage? Her supplemental coverage? Should I go to the hospital with those tomorrow?"

"I took care of sending that information when I sent the Medical POA."

A sigh of sadness escaped. "Poor Lillian. She's so alone."

Dee reached over and squeezed my hand. "No, she's not. She's got you."

"And you," I said.

My sister nodded. "And the sexy detective across the street."

I groaned. "Let's not talk about Zack."

"Oh, you're not getting off that easy," she drawled, her eyes glinting with humor.

Before I could protest again, Baxter gave a bark and growl, his gaze fixed on the gate. Both of us turned to see what the dog was alerting us about. The gate opened, and our sister, Brooke, walked into the yard.

"I need wine," she called. "Bottles and bottles of wine."

I pushed out of my chair and hurried over to hug my sister. "I'll get another bottle. It's good to see you. I haven't seen you in forever."

Brooke hugged me back. "The hospital is trying to kill me, I swear."

"Take my chair. I'll grab another."

I retrieved another bottle of merlot and a wine glass from my kitchen. When I returned, I set the bottle on the table and pulled a third lounger near the first two, which were both filled by my favorite people in the world.

"I couldn't wait," Brooke said, holding up my empty glass. "Sorry. You want your glass back?"

"Keep it. I have another."

"Am I interrupting something?" Brooke asked with a frown. "You both look so serious."

"Nope," Dee said. "I was just pressing our much, *much* older sister for deets on the sexy cop across the street."

Brooke's face lit up with a smile. "*Really*?" She filled the wine glass to the rim and said, "Do I know him? Is he cute? Tell me everything."

Brooke's excited—and loud—voice got Baxter riled up. He began to bark and howl at the foot of her chair.

"See?" I said, arching an eyebrow. "Even Baxter knows it none of your business...either of yours. And I'm not that much older."

"Oh, come on. I haven't been on a date in forever," Brooke complained. "Let me live vicariously through you."

"By your own choice," I observed.

Brooke downed her wine. "Honestly, I haven't found an interesting man I want to date."

"Interesting woman, perhaps?" Dee asked.

"Nope. I'm all for dicks."

Dee and I snorted wine out of our noses.

"Well, I'm glad we cleared that up," I said, still laughing.

"I don't know how we got on the subject of my appreciation of penis power, but I want to hear about the cop. Let's start with the name," Brooke said.

"Zack Noles," Dee supplied.

"Dee! You have a big mouth," I said, glaring at her.

"Oh, I know Detective Noles," Brooke said, a sly smile on her lips. "There's hardly a female in the ER who doesn't know him. In fact, most of them try to be the one who gets to help him first."

I frowned. "I don't understand. Why is he in the ER so much?"

Brooke refilled her wine glass before speaking. "Well, first, the man's been shot at least two times, maybe more. I don't know. Plus, he's usually around when an arrest goes sideways and the perp ends up in our ER."

"Perp?" Dee said with a laugh. "Listen to you...all the cop lingo."

My heart sputtered and skipped a few beats. My stomach fell at the mention that Zack had been shot on the job...at least, I assumed it was on the job.

"Anyway, he's a darling," Brooke said. "Always so nice to the staff. Of course, I remember him from our UT days. He's aged well." She looked at me and wrinkled her brow. "Are you okay? You look pale."

"Zack's been shot before?"

"Yeah, but not near any major organs," Brooke said flippantly. "Shoulder once and leg once—at least those are the ones I was involved with. We always have to fight with him to get him to stay once he's fixed up. Usually, he's ready to go."

I felt sick to my stomach. I'd never given any thought to his job being dangerous. "I had no idea. I mean, that's stupid. Of course, I know police work can be risky, but I hadn't given it much thought."

"So, why are we talking about Zack Noles? I've lost track of the conversation," Brooke said and then drained her wine glass.

"He's Andi's sexy neighbor," Dee replied.

"Oh, really?" Brooke said, her gaze narrowing on me.

"Yep, and when you got here, I was just asking her about him." Dee twisted in her chair until she faced me. After propping her elbows on the arm of the chair and placing her chin in her cupped hands, she smiled. "Tell us everything. What was seeing him again like? Did he mention that night you left the bar with him? Does he still call you Princess? Spill."

"Yeah, I want to hear this, too," Brooke said. She leaned forward as though those six inches closer to me would somehow make it easier for her to hear.

My stomach clenched. "Nothing to tell. I've seen him twice. Once last night when he came into Lillian's house to see why the front door was open, and then today, when he came by my office."

Dee popped upright. "You didn't tell me he came by the office."

I slumped. "He was just being friendly. We went by the hospital to check on Lillian and then got called to her house because of the break-in."

Dee held up her hand, palm out. "Stop. What break-in?"

I sighed and went through the story of the open back door, the empty safe, and the missing silver. While I'd been telling the story, Baxter must have detected how stressed I was. He jumped into my lap and settled down, as did my anxiety as I stroked him.

"That's horrible," Brooke said.

"Yes, it is. I think what freaks me out is knowing

whoever did it was probably in Lillian's house while I was there last night."

"Yikes," Dee said, and then she smiled. "But at least you had a strong cop to defend you."

I rolled her eyes. "Nothing happening there."

"You never did tell us what happened in college between the two of you," Dee said.

Sweat pooled in the palms of my hands. A cold drop of perspiration rolled down my back. I hoped my eagled-eyed sisters didn't notice the slight tremor in my hand as I lifted my wine glass with a silent wish they'd move off the subject.

Brooke tapped my knee for attention. "You know, I've always wondered about you two. A couple of times, I noticed Detective Noles studying me when he was in the ER. I sort of figured it was because I look so much like you."

I shrugged. "Honestly, I don't remember a lot of that evening. Henry and I had had a big argument and broke up. Zack came in looking all sexy and hot, and then he was beside me, talking to me, making me feel so much better." I paused, lost in the memory.

"I remember that night well. You were gloomy on the ride home. Then, when you woke up the next day, you didn't say much, but Dee and I assumed you'd slept with him."

I nodded. "Can we leave it at that? A fling in my past. That was it."

Dee arched her eyebrows. "Isn't it strange how our pasts can come charging into the present and change everything?"

Seven

As I'd done yesterday, I took Baxter with me to the office the next day. Robin was ready for her temporary canine assistant. An extra water bowl and a dog bed now graced the corner of her office, as well as mine.

"Hey, precious," Robin cooed. "Did you have a good night?"

"Aww," I replied with a fake sniff. "You really care about me."

Robin laughed. "Well, sure, but I'm talking to the cutie in your arms." She wiggled her fingers. "Hand him over. The office staff has filled out his walk schedule for today, so we're good to go." She took the dog from me. "Plus, you have to get your visual media finished for the board meeting."

I frowned. "I worry that Baxter is too much of a distraction for the office. I know he's a cutie, but I don't want him to keep the staff from getting their work done."

"Actually, he's not a problem at all. He's more an inducement to get their work done. No walking the dog if you're behind on work."

"Okay, but it might be hard to explain that incentive to HR. Speaking of behind on work, I'm guilty. I'll get the graphics to you shortly."

An hour later, there was a knock at my door. I frowned as I saw Robin's head coming around the edge of the door.

"Someone is here to see you. He doesn't have an appointment but says he's here to take Baxter?"

"The hell he is." I stood. "No one is taking that dog. What's this person's name?"

"Randall Branson. Says Lillian is his grandmother."

"Interesting." Even as my brain began to run possible scenarios for what Lillian's grandson really wanted, I was slipping my feet back into my high heels. I'd gotten used to wearing heels and was thankful I'd worn my seriously kickass pair. There was something about standing tall in kickass heels that gave me a sense of confidence. "Send him in."

Robin opened my office door wider and a man in his mid-to-late twenties walked in. His khaki slacks, while clean and pressed, were a smidge too tight and a few years of out of style, as though they'd been pulled from the back of the closet. The sleeves of his white oxford shirt were rolled to his elbows, exposing his forearms, which lacked muscular definition. I had a thing for muscular forearms and his were sadly lacking. His dark hair had been pulled into a man bun, drawing attention to his thin, drawn face. The smile he gave me held no warmth or much friendliness. I would swear the temperature in the room dropped twenty degrees with his presence.

"Ms. Carmichael. I'm Randall, Lillian's grandson," he said as he walked across my office with his hand extended.

I walked from behind my desk to meet the man halfway. I felt obliged to take the proffered hand, but at the same time, a nervous chill ran down my spine. After the shortest handshake in my life, I broke the connection. It took everything in my power not to rub my palm against my skirt. "Mr. Branson, what can I do for you?"

The oily smile remained. "I heard about my grandmother's fall. I promised her I would take Baxter if anything happened to her. Her neighbor told me you'd taken him. Thank you for your generosity, but I'll take him off your hands now. Maybe you could ask your staff to help me load him into my car? I'd appreciate it. Where is that sweet boy?" His gaze flashed around the room.

I moved back behind the desk. "I'm sorry... Randall, is it? There seems to be a misunderstanding. Lillian gave Baxter to me and said nothing about you coming to get him. Therefore, he will be staying with me. And how did you know he would be in my office?"

His jaw hardened, as did his expression. "A neighbor told me. Now, I'm a busy man and don't have all day to stand around. Just bring me the dog and I'll be on my way."

"That's not going to happen. Now, since you're such a busy, busy man, you may go about your day knowing your grandmother's precious pet is well taken care of." I gestured toward the door. "Show yourself out."

If looks could kill, I'd have been dropping to my carpet. Luckily for me, I'd survived many a death stare from one sister or the other. Today was no exception. I remained standing behind my desk, refusing to be bullied by the man-child.

Lillian's grandson huffed. "You'll be hearing from my lawyer."

I nodded. "That's fine. My assistant can provide all the information your lawyer will need to contact me." Setting both hands flat on the desk, I leaned toward him, a hateful glare on my face.

He took a couple of steps back.

"Lillian is very special to me. Her expressed desires will be carried out as she wanted. I am also a lawyer, Mr. Branson. I have unimpeachable witnesses that heard her tell me, not ask me, but tell me to take her dog and keep him until she got home. So, don't fuck with me. You won't like the outcome." I gestured toward the door, proud of myself that I didn't use the middle finger to point. "Get out. I have serious work to do."

After a solid minute of a glaring stare-down, he whirled around and marched out of my office, slamming my door with his exit.

I dropped into my chair, my heart racing. *Don't fuck with me?* Where had that tidbit come from? My hands were still clenched into angry fists when Robin stuck her head into the office.

"Don't fuck with me?" Robin laughed. "I have never heard you use that word in my life."

"I know, I know." I sighed and leaned heavily against the back of my chair. "He just made me so mad."

"I thought he was creepy."

I nodded. "I wouldn't put it past him to be the one who took things from Lillian's house."

"You think? Why would he want Baxter so bad?"

"No clue. Speaking of which, where is he?"

"Hidden in accounting. Sheila has him stashed under her desk."

I chuckled. "Good. Since my concentration is shot at the moment, I think I'll head to the hospital. Lillian's case manager called earlier, and they're moving her to the rehab floor. I want to go up and make sure she's settled."

"Send what you've completed, and I'll start working on the graphics."

"Thanks."

And once again, I was thankful to have found such an incredible assistant.

Once I arrived at the hospital, I discovered that Lillian had been moved up to the eighth floor, room 804. As I neared the room, I heard Lillian's laugh, which made my heart happy and my mouth smile.

Then I heard a deeper laugh, and her stomach

clenched. I knew that laugh. Zack was here. Maybe I should leave and come back later.

Sweat collected in my palms. It was just like when I'd been in high school, and a cute boy would speak to me. One would think at my age, I'd be past adolescent reactions.

But my kickass heels gave me the confidence to step into the open doorway. What I saw made me smile. Zack was acting out something, using his pointed finger like a gun. Lillian's hands covered her mouth as she laughed.

"And then, he wet his pants," Zack said.

"Oh my." Lillian giggled.

"Yeah, I put him in a patrol car. I wasn't letting him sit on my back seat."

"Sounds like I missed quite a story," I said, kind of sorry I had missed it. "How are you feeling, Lillian?"

"Like an old fool. Come here and give me a hug. I want to hear about how Baxter is doing."

"I should be going," Zack said.

"No, stay," I said. "I don't want to run you off."

"Stay," Lillian echoed. "You've only just gotten here." She held out her hand to him, which he took. Then she held out her other hand to me, and of course, I had to take her hand too. "My two heroes. I might not be here if not for you."

I squeezed her hand. "Good neighbors. Everyone needs them." She shifted her gaze to Zack. "What have you two been discussing?"

Zack released Lillian's hand. He dragged a chair

over to the side of the bed and gestured for me to take a seat.

"Those shoes look deadly," he said with an arched brow.

"Thanks." I kicked my foot up and turned my foot from one side to the other as though admiring my shoe. "Hell to run in, though."

He laughed. Lillian giggled.

"The prices we women pay to look good," Lillian said.

Zack cleared his throat and ran his hand through his hair. He sighed loudly.

"Oh, dear. You've got bad news to tell me," Lillian said. "I know you, Zack. Just say it quick."

"Someone broke into your house and, we think, stole some items."

Lillian looked at me. "Did you know?"

I nodded with a frown. "I was with Zack when he got the call?"

"When?"

"Yesterday, around noon," he said. His face grew serious. "Lillian, any ideas who'd do that?"

Lillian wouldn't meet either of their gazes.

I retook Lillian's hand. "Lillian, you have to trust us."

"What's missing?" Lillian asked in a rasping voice.

"Until you can get back to the house and give us a full accounting, we won't know for sure." Zack's mouth drew into a line. "I think you have an idea of who did this."

She shook her head but refused to meet either Zack's or my gaze.

"Lillian," I said softly. "The night of your fall, who was at your house?"

"What makes you think I had company?"

I squeezed Lillian's hand. "I know you. There's no way you'd go to bed and leave a sink of dirty dishes. Plus, there were too many for just you. Can I guess?" I shifted my gaze from my stubborn neighbor over to Zack and then back. "Lillian, I know you trust Zack and me." I drew a deep breath and said, "It was your grandson, Randall, right?"

A tear dripped from Lillian's eye. Her lips tightened. I guessed she was fighting the tears and the need to tell someone what really happened. In my heart, I just knew it was the man who'd visited my office this morning, and I swore, if he intentionally hurt this wonderful woman, I was going to use my high heels to teach him a lesson.

Zack patted Lillian's hand. "If this involves your grandson, I promise I'll do what I can to help him," he said. "But I have to know what's going on."

The tear on Lillian's cheek was joined by a second one and then a third. "Yes, yes. Randall came to dinner. I haven't seen him in so long, maybe five years." She sniffed. "When my daughter died, he didn't come for the funeral. He's just so angry at me, at life, at everything."

"So, what really happened when you broke your leg?" I asked softly. I ached for my neighbor while fury at Randall raged in my gut.

"It really was like I said, or close enough. Randall had come to dinner. I asked him to stay the night. I was in the kitchen, on the stool, trying to put a heavy pitcher back into the cabinet. As I slid it in, the stool shifted on the rug. I reached for something to hold on to, but as I fell, I saw Randall watching me."

"Did he push you?" I asked. I forced my tone to be calm and caring, but emotionally, I was far from both.

Lillian shook her head. "No, but he wouldn't help me either. He said the sooner I die, the sooner he gets what's coming to him."

Zack fisted his hand. "I'd like to give him what's coming to him and hard."

"After my daughter, his mother, died, I changed my will and set up a trust." Her gaze slid over to me. "Your sister was wonderful to help me."

I smiled. "Yeah, Dee's pretty special."

"Have you read the trust?"

I shook her head. "No. She showed me the medical and financial powers of attorney you gave me, but I didn't need to see the rest. Dee is good at keeping client information private."

"Well, Randall insisted on getting a copy of my will. I explained that I have everything in a trust now, but I don't think he understood what that meant. The last thing he said was for me to quit acting like an idiot and get off the floor, and we'd continue our talk in the morning. Then he went to bed."

"With you on the floor?" My tone was furious, colored with disgust at her grandson.

Lillian shut her eyes. Obviously, telling this story was embarrassing and draining for Lillian, but I knew Zack needed all the information. I appreciated his letting me take the lead with this discussion instead of being all cop-like and hitting Lillian with a ton of cop questions.

"Yes," Lillian finally said with a long sigh. "He didn't know I'd broken anything. His mother was such a drama queen about everything, so I'm sure he learned to ignore her, just like he did me."

"You're no drama queen," Zack said in a growly voice.

"I know that, and you know that, but Randall doesn't." She sighed again as if this story was wringing her dry. "I tried to get on my feet for a while. Finally, I gave up and called you." She looked at me. "Thank you for coming over."

"Lillian, I'll always be around when you need me. I swear. I'm not going anywhere."

"I hate to ask this, Lillian," Zack said, "but was your grandson still in the house when the ambulance took you away?"

She nodded, her expression drawn and sad.

"Is it possible he's the one who set off your alarm yesterday?"

She shrugged. "Maybe. Do you have any idea what's missing?"

Zack looked at me and gestured for me to say something. My thought was, *Thanks, pal*. I dropped my chin to my chest and blew out a breath. "Your silver cabinet's empty," I said. "And your vases and art

ASSETS

pieces from the living room. Your safe was open, but I don't know what was in there."

"Not much," Lillian said. "Maybe a thousand dollars or so for emergencies. Mostly I kept important papers in there."

"Your trust papers?"

"Yes." She sighed again.

"Do you have any idea of the value of things he took?"

"You don't know he took them," she insisted, obviously still hopeful her grandson wasn't the thief.

I pursed her lips. "Okay, do you have any idea of the value of the missing items?"

"I'm tired," Lillian said. "I need to sleep."

She shut her eyes, effectively shutting us out.

I stood and placed a kiss on Lillian's forehead. "Get some rest, Lillian. Baxter needs you to come home." I saw Lillian's lips twist upward in just the tiniest of movements at the mention of her dog. I couldn't blame her. He was stealing hearts all over Dallas.

With a tilt of my head for Zack to follow me, I walked into the hall with him close on my heels.

"Well, her grandson sounds like he's going to miss out on the Grandson of the Year award," Zack said.

He put his hand on the small of my back and led me to an empty seating area. The heat of his broad palm burned thought my jacket and shirt, warming my back like a heating pad. I was sure the rest of me would heat as fast if he touched my other places.

97

And yes, I realized the totally inappropriate timing of my thoughts.

"I guess I should confess," I said as we sat.

"Well, my day just got more interesting. Do I need to frisk you before or after you confess? I've got handcuffs if you're into that."

I slugged his bicep with my fist. "Ouch. That hurt. Do you have steel armor under that jacket?"

He grinned, and my stomach and heart both clenched, leaving me without a breath.

"You're good for my ego," he said. "Now, confession time. I'm listening."

"Randall Branson showed up in my office today, demanding that I hand over Baxter."

A deep furrow formed on the cop's brow. "I admit, I wasn't expecting that confession. I'm assuming you told him to drop dead."

"Not in so many words, but I may have told him, 'Don't fuck with me. You won't win.'"

Zack nodded and chuckled. "I bet you scared the piss out of the guy."

"He left, but he says he's getting a lawyer to force me to give him the dog."

"But why? I admit, Baxter is a cute dog, but given Baxter's age and the last time Lillian saw her grandson, I suspect he never met the dog until this week."

"Good question. Doesn't matter. The dog is going nowhere with him." I stood. "I have to get back to work. Nice running into you."

"Dinner?"

"Excuse me?"

"Have dinner with me tonight."

I shook my head. "Sounds nice, but I'm not leaving Baxter alone, not even for a night. Randall seemed a little desperate this morning to get his hands on him, and I don't know why. Until I understand what's going on, the dog goes where I go."

"Where is the little guy now?"

"Baxter?"

"No, Randall," Zack said sarcastically. "Of course, I mean Baxter."

We began walking toward the elevator. "That little boy has an army of corporate women protecting him. When I left, he was hiding in the accounting department under a desk." I smiled. "He's safe there. Not one of those women will let him out of sight."

"Good. Then it's settled. Dinner will be at your house."

I stopped walking and looked at him with an arched brow. "It's settled?"

"Well, yeah...all but the timing."

"How do you know I want to have dinner with you?" My heart raced. Did I want to have dinner with him? *Yes* battled *No* in my brain. What scared me was that no man had ever touched my soul like he had, which is why I'd run so many years ago. Did I really want to reopen that door?

We were on the elevator alone, no one listening to our conversation, thank goodness, because I was sure my face flamed red when Zack whispered in my ear, "I remember how you smell when you're turned on, Princess. It's like nectar to a bee, and I'm the bee." He gently bit my ear. "I'll see you at seven," he whispered, straightening as the elevator doors slid opened. "I'll bring everything. You don't have to do a thing," he said, and exited the elevator car into the hospital lobby.

How I made it from the hospital lobby to my car on quaking knees and shaky legs would forever mystify me. My heart galloped, not out of my chest, but it felt like it wanted to. My brain was dizzy and fuzzy. When I finally got to my car, I dropped behind the steering wheel with a gasp for air. *What just happened?*

Eight

"I don't know what I've gotten us into, Baxter," I confided on the drive home. "Am I making a mistake letting him back in?"

Baxter yipped excitedly. I decided to take that as encouragement that I was making the right decision. Damn, I appreciated his support.

"What do I wear?" I glanced over at the tiny dog in the doggie car seat. "Jeans? Maybe a pair of yoga pants, like I don't care what he thinks?"

The dog panted back at me.

"See? You were giving good answers until now."

My phone rang through the car's Bluetooth.

"Hello?"

"It's me," Dee said.

"Hey, me. What's going on?"

"Um, I need to talk to you."

"Okay, talk."

"Not on the phone. Can I come over?"

"Um...." I hesitated. I didn't want my sisters

making a big deal out of Zack making dinner tonight. On the other hand, I had nothing to be embarrassed about. But I dreaded the inquisition when they found out.

"You have a date tonight or something?" Dee asked.

I winced, even though no one could see me but Baxter. "Something like that."

"*Ohhh,* tell me more. Who with? I know, I know. The hunky cop from your past. Am I right? I'm right, aren't I? Woot, woot. Andi's got a date with someone other than the stick-up-his-butt Richard."

"Would you stop it?" I pulled to a stop in my drive and laughed. "Sorry to burst your bubble, but it's not a romantic hookup. I'm sure Zack just wants to talk about Lillian's house and stuff."

My sister hooted with laughter. "I wish I could see your face right now. I bet you're flushed with little drops of sweat on your brow."

"Screw you." I dabbed at the brow sweat. "You don't know everything."

"Girl, I know when you're lying, so give it up."

"Fine. We're having dinner. Are you happy?"

"Ecstatic. What are you making?"

"I'm not making dinner. He is."

"Way to keep him in line," Dee said, her tone admiring.

"So, what did you want to talk to me about? I have an hour or so."

"Not on the phone. Lunch, tomorrow?"

"Sure. Sounds great. Want to meet at Island Salad House around eleven?"

"Perfect. See you then."

Once my sister was off the line, I pulled my Benz around to the rear garage and parked. "Mighty mysterious, right?"

Baxter yipped.

"Yeah, that's what I think, too."

I settled on jeans and a white Oxford shirt. I debated shoes versus sandals versus barefoot because, you know, it was my house and tonight wasn't a big deal. I settled on slide-on sandals that could be dumped easily.

Promptly at seven, my doorbell rang. Baxter leapt up from where he was sleeping in my blue wingback chair—telling him to stay off my furniture was a waste of breath—and flew toward the door, barking the entire way. I rolled her eyes, but I couldn't contain the grin on my face as I followed the fierce defender of my home to the door.

I opened the door and smiled. Zack held an enormous brown paper bag in one hand and two bottles of wine in the other.

"Who needs a doorbell with Baxter around?" he said.

Mouth-watering aromas of Italian food drifted from the bag. My stomach growled its compliments to the chef.

"Hungry?" he asked with a grin.

I laughed with a shake of my head and took the wine. "Let me help. It smells delicious. DeLuca's?"

"Of course. Only the best."

I tilted my head toward the rear of my house. "Inside or outside?"

"Inside, and I want the grand tour. Just seeing your place is giving me tons of ideas for mine."

I headed into the dining room. "This work?"

"Naw. Too formal. I bet you have a great little area in your kitchen."

With an eye roll, I led him to my kitchen and its cozy eating nook.

"See? I just knew you had something like this," he said.

"Bossy, much?" I asked with a grin.

"I thought you liked it when I was bossy...at least, that's my memory."

I sighed and tried to deflect. "Open the wine while I get some glasses. Let's get this conversation over."

While he was setting out the lasagna, breadsticks, and salad on the small table, I retrieved two Waterford crystal wine glasses from my hutch.

His eyebrows arched as he took the glass I offered. "Fancy."

I shrugged. "What's the good of having crystal if you don't use it? If it breaks, I'll buy another. It does no good sitting on a shelf day after day, year after year. Besides, I honestly think wine tastes better out of a nice glass."

"Works for me." He filled both glasses with a ruby-red wine and gently tapped his glass to mine. The delicate crystal sang. "Cheers."

"Cheers." I took a sip and smiled. "Wow, this is excellent."

"I have grown up from the beer and cheap booze I drank during my college days."

I winced. "I'm sorry. I didn't mean it the way it sounded. I'm sure we've both changed since those days. I'll grab some plates and silverware."

Rather than risk a comment about fancy dishes, I opted for my super casual stoneware. I set plates along with the everyday flatware on the table. It wasn't that I didn't have fine china and a full set of sterling silver flatware we could have used. I did. When my sisters and I had turned eighteen, my paternal grandmother had gifted each of my sisters and me with complete sets. But for tonight, all that would remain in storage.

Anyway, if Zack's reaction to the crystal was any indication, bone china and sterling flatware would have been off-putting.

Once our plates were loaded with the mouth-watering lasagna, and we'd sat at the table, I pointed my fork at him. "Okay, say whatever it is you want to say. I know you're itching to get it out on the table."

He wiped his mouth on the napkin from his lap and said, "Why did you sneak away in the middle of the night? That's bugged me for years."

I set my fork on my plate and took a sip of wine. My gut clenched, and my throat clogged. How did I tell a man that the way he'd knocked my socks off that night had been unlike anything I'd ever experienced? Wouldn't that be giving away too much information?

"I don't know. Embarrassed? Unsure of how to handle the situation? I always wondered why you wanted me? How was I different from my sisters? Or you were with me because I was the available sister." I dipped my head. "As you became aware that night, my sexual, um, experience had been limited."

His mouth dropped. "The available one?" He sighed, set his fork on his plate, and took my hand. "You have no idea how much beer I had to drink just to get up the courage to talk to you that first night at the Orange Cactus. I didn't stopped thinking about you all through the holiday. I was supposed to be thinking about offense plays and defense for the Sugar Bowl, and all I really wanted was to kiss you again. And then that spring when I came in with the baseball team? I walked straight past everyone, including your sisters, to get to you. I was crushing on you for months."

"You were?" My mind whirled in confusion My heart leaped into my throat. "A crush on me?"

"Yes, you. Not Dee. Not Brooke. You. Dee and I were in class together that semester. She's the one who told me that you and Henry had split up and that you were headed to that bar that night."

I leaned back in my chair in astonishment. "Dee set me up?"

"I don't know about that. All I can say is she let me know where you'd be and when."

"Did Dee know that…um…?" I waved my hand between us.

"That I was crushing hard?" He chuckled. "I don't know. It was a conversation with a group of people, not just me, so I can't say that she knew. Probably didn't." He turned my hand over until he could lace our fingers. "I was seriously wounded when I woke up and you were gone."

"I'm sorry." I placed my hand over our clasped fingers. "I…I just didn't know how to deal with…" I shrugged my lack of ability to find the words to explain my reaction to him.

"I don't understand. I called. Dee answered and she told me you were back with Henry and I should probably leave you alone. How could we have that kind of connection and you walk away? And don't tell me you didn't feel it. You had to. There's no way I was alone in my reaction."

"Zack, you know I was pretty much a virgin that night."

"And that confused me even more. How? You're stunningly beautiful. You'd had a boyfriend, you know, the one you went back to after me."

I dropped my chin to my chest. I was embarrassed by my actions and this uncomfortable discussion.

He pulled me out of my chair and into his lap. I put my face on his shoulder, but tipped my face so our gazes met. "Talk to me, Princess. This is important."

"I was totally inexperienced. I mean, I'd been with Henry, but we hadn't had sex, and now you're going to ask why." I sighed and looked in his eyes. "It never felt right. I know that sounds crazy, but in my heart, I didn't want to sleep with...any guy...until you."

"Why me?"

I broke eye contact, but he caught my chin in his fingers and made me look at him.

"Why did you sleep with me?"

"Because I was sure you'd been with lots of girls and knew what to do. I knew what the books said. I knew what I'd read in romances, and that's what I wanted, I guess. A guy to sweep me off my feet and take the lead."

"Yeah, I call bullshit. You're not a girl who allows herself to be swept off her feet and lets a man direct her actions. You want to tell me the truth now?"

Between his hard chest and my wall of lies, I was trapped. I slipped back into my chair and brushed my hair behind my ear. "I don't know what you want me to say?"

"The truth, darling. Why did you go home with me that night?"

I sighed. "I'd never met a guy who could make me feel like you did. Not Henry. Not any of the guys I dated. When you kissed me in the parking lot after our birthday party in December, it was like a switch flipped inside. I sound crazy." I chuckled. "Just mark that night as me taking something I wanted."

He took my hand. "You aren't crazy. I felt that too. When I woke up and you were gone? Well, that killed me."

I huffed out my disbelief. "Sure, it did, Mr. Popularity. For the rest of the semester, every time our paths crossed, you had your arm around a different girl. You seemed to have sprung back."

He picked up his fork. "That's because you broke my heart. I wasn't letting anyone else do that to me."

"Did I really?"

"Yeah." He set his fork down again. "A little. I thought we'd really connected that night, but when you were gone in the morning, I decided it was all one-sided."

"Why didn't you reach out to me sometime in the past thirteen years?"

"And say what? 'Hey, Andi! Remember me from college? Wanna go on a date?'"

"Sure, why not?"

He shook his head, but the dejection on his face broke my heart.

"You moved across the street from me. Why haven't you walked over and knocked on my damn door?"

"You want the truth, honey? I don't think I could have stood being rejected again."

"Oh. I'm sorry. I didn't know. After all the women at college, not to mention the social media pictures of you and a parade of models during your NFL days, I assumed I was a night from your past. I didn't even know if you'd remember me."

"Remember you? Every woman I dated couldn't hold a candle to you."

I dipped my head with a blush. "I don't believe you, but I'll take the compliment."

"So, where do we stand? Are you single?"

I winced. "Single, yes, but I have been seeing someone."

"Ha. My point exactly. Is it serious?"

I shook my head. "No, in fact. I was thinking the other day that I should end it."

He smiled. "I think you should, too."

I tilted my head and smiled. "Oh yeah? And then?" My heart pounded loudly as I waited for his reply; I was nervous I wouldn't hear him over the racket my heart was making. But mostly, I was afraid to hope, afraid to dream of a future with him.

"And then we date and see where this goes."

I released the breath I'd been holding. "Exclusive?"

"Definitely, Princess. I'll be honest. I know you're far out of my league, but I can't get you out of my soul. You've ingrained yourself."

I smiled and ran my hand along his jaw. "I want to try, Zack. You've been the only man I wanted for years."

Again, he pulled me over and into his lap—this time for a long, deep kiss. "You just keep thinking that, Princess."

While we were cleaning up after dinner, he asked a million questions about my house renovations, including the names of all the subcontractors I'd used. I promised to put together a list and send it to him. I knew Robin had all the information so getting him a list would be easy. Besides, it gave me joy to help him.

"I never asked, why did you buy the Skaggs's old place?" I asked. "I respect a challenge as much as the next person, but wow. You've undertaken a big one."

"Ethyl and Raymond Skaggs were family...well, distant family. She was my mother's great-aunt. I remember coming over here when I was just a kid. I thought this was a neighborhood of mansions, and I grew up dreaming of living in this area. After both of the Skaggs died and their children had no interest whatsoever in the old place, I bought it. Got a great deal because of the condition, but I knew what I was getting into."

"I'm glad. I love these old homes. Did you apply for one of our foundation's grants for houses in this area?"

He frowned. "What grants?"

I explained about the foundation's grant program, but also about the catch. Houses renovated through grants had to be open for an annual Christmas tour that raised money for additional grants to renovate other homes in the area.

"You bet I'm interested. What do I need to know?"

"I'll bring home the papers tomorrow night for you, okay?"

He gave me a slow, sexy smile that sent my heart racing. "Dinner two nights in a row? Do I have to like sleep with someone to get one of these grants?"

My heart twittered and the area between my

thighs got suddenly damp. "You don't have to, but..." I shrugged. "It never hurts."

He laughed and pulled me into a tight embrace. "I'll try to remember all my tricks."

As I shook my head, Baxter charged into the kitchen. Apparently done with his dinner, the tiny general was ready to order his troops to play.

Zack threw a ball out the door into the yard, and Baxter raced to retrieve it.

"You enjoy dogs," I said as I saw the pleasure playing with Baxter brought him.

"I do."

"I didn't think I'd like having Baxter underfoot, but he's great company."

"You're going to miss him when Lillian gets home."

"Or maybe I'll kidnap him and keep him here with me."

Zack laughed. "I'd have to arrest you for dognapping."

"Does that involve frisking and handcuffs?" I coyly batted my eyelashes at him.

"Total body cavity search," he said in a voice that betrayed how much he liked the idea.

"Hmm. What other crimes require a body cavity search?"

We'd relocated to my deck while Zack had been playing with Baxter. I found a seat on one of the loungers. Zack threw the ball one more time, then slipped behind me, placing me snuggly between his thick, muscular thighs. Then, he leaned close to my ear and whispered, "For a career criminal like you, a total body cavity search might be needed nightly."

His hot breath and whispered words sent goose bumps popping on my arms. Chills rolled down my spine, vertebra by vertebra. I turned until my face was angled toward him. "May I suggest you start with my mouth?"

So, he did. Long, deep, wet kisses that had me squirming in his lap. Hands roamed. Mine moved up and down his chest and over his shoulders. His swept along my sides to my hips and then back up to my breasts. His low, guttural moans vibrated my chest and invaded my soul. His thick cock pressed into my side, making me hungry for him in my bed.

Memories from years ago flooded my brain. His mouth kissing and licking its way down my body until he found my core. I'd left more behind than just my V card. I'd left behind my heart. I'd always believed so, but now, at this moment, back in his arms, I knew it to be fact.

"I've got to go," he murmured against my lips.

"No," I whined. "Don't go. Stay." My arms tightened around him.

He kissed my forehead. "I can't. I wish I could. I'd give anything to stay, but I can't tonight. I've got to get to work. But before I leave, look at something for me."

I sat back with a resigned sigh. "If it's a picture of your cock, I'd rather see the real deal."

He chuckled. "Oh, honey. You'll be seeing that

up close and personal real soon." He nudged me with his rigid dick. "Scoot. I need to stand up."

"So, what you're saying is if I don't move, you can't leave and you'll have to stay here with me? You give me no incentive to move."

He grinned and kissed me. "I've missed that mouth of yours. Now, scoot."

"See? Bossy, just like I said."

He chuckled and kissed me again, which led to another round of deep kisses, until he gently pushed me away and gave me a warm smile. "Keep that up, and I'll be late."

"Fine," I said and moved in, but he just laughed as he picked me up and moved me to the foot of the lounger

He slipped from the chair and grabbed his coat from the back of the other chair. From an inside pocket, he pulled a photograph and handed it to her. "Look familiar?"

I studied it. "Randall Branson. Mug shot?"

He nodded. "Lillian's grandson has a long and not-so-glamorous criminal history. Burglaries, theft by receiving, public intoxication, vandalism, and one count of DUI. He's got a juvie record, too, but it's sealed and not really important. I don't like him around here, especially not around you or Lillian. See if you can get her to tell you more about the night she fell." His mouth tightened in anger. "That little cock-sucker went to bed and left his grandmother on the kitchen floor. Even if that isn't illegal, it's despicable."

"Agreed." I stood and wrapped my arms around his waist. "I enjoyed tonight."

His eyes warmed as he gazed down at me. "Me, too. The first of many, I hope."

That look. It'd slayed me years ago, and I felt its pull deep inside. I felt the heat of my cheeks as a blush climbed my neck. "Yeah. The first of many. Be safe tonight."

He kissed the tip of my nose. "Nothing dangerous going on tonight."

"Are you always on nights?"

"Naw. I'm on a special project. A big bad deal is going down. Not sure when. Not sure how. Not sure who. We just know it's coming, so I spend my nights in bars you've never heard of, and have never gone in...nor will you, if I have my say."

"I might have been inside a rough bar before. Try me. Give me some names."

"No way. Knowing you and your sisters, you three would go to one or two just to see how bad it can be. I can see the three of you getting yourselves into a heap of trouble."

"You do know me too well."

He gave me a quick kiss. "I really have to run. Baxter," he called.

The tiny pup ran from inside the house with a yip. He caught the dog and swung him into his arms. "Now, you keep this lady safe, you hear?"

Baxter licked Zack's nose.

"Good. We have a deal."

I watched Zack with the dog. Every nook and

cranny inside me exploded with joy and happiness. I'd never felt anything like this before. Pieces of a life that had felt scattered fell into place. Contentment draped over me like a warm blanket.

Was what I felt because of the dog or the man?

Nine

I'd been hunched over my desk working since six
a.m., trying to get some projects off to Robin.
When my phone rang, the startling old-timey ring I
set as my ringtone broke the quiet I'd been enjoying.
Apparently, the sound disturbed Baxer, too, since he
leapt up and barked at the noise. I picked up my
phone to read the caller ID. As soon as I did, I wished
I hadn't. RICHARD LONG flashed on the screen. I
blew out a long breath. I knew I had to deal with the
situation. It wasn't fair to him, or Zack, for that
matter. He'd laid his heart on the line for me last
night. It was time for me to do what I'd been thinking
about for a while.

"Hello, Richard."

"Andrea. I was beginning to think you were
avoiding me."

Ugh. He always took things personally, even
when they didn't have a thing to do with him. Plus,

he considered my "little job" was more of a figure-head position than one that did real work, so he could never understand why I wasn't at his beck and call at all times.

"No, not at all. Just busy."

"I'd like to have dinner tonight with you. Maybe go to The Marble Mansion for steaks?"

The Marble Mansion was the hottest restaurant in Dallas. Its popularity made getting reservations just shy of impossible.

"The Marble Mansion? How did you get reserva-tions? I heard they were booked out for months."

He clicked his tongue, and the sound grated on me like fingernails on a blackboard. "It's not what you know, but who you know in this city. Besides, we haven't been out in a couple of weeks. You're taking that little job of yours way too seriously. You have a staff. You should use them better."

I gritted my teeth. My staff was excellent, that was true, but I'd never ask them to do something I wouldn't. Yeah, it was time to cut this smelly fish loose. If only my mother hadn't drilled manners into me....

"Tonight? What time? I'll rearrange my schedule."

Not surprisingly, I didn't have any desire to see him...tonight or any night. Plus, I didn't enjoy conflict and feared breaking it off would bring the kind of uncomfortable situation I dreaded.

Besides, I was supposed to see Zack tonight.

Unlike with Richard, the thought of seeing Zack made all my internal lights flash. Just thinking of Zack made me smile. I'd have to call Zack and explain the situation. He'd understand. Heck, he'd probably be glad I was getting myself out of the situation with Richard.

"Why don't I pick you up at seven? Your office?"

When I'd first gotten my driver's license and car, I found a freedom I was reluctant to hand over to anyone else. Besides, I wouldn't put it past him to be mad enough to leave me stranded once he understood I was breaking things off. "Why don't I meet you there? I have a few things to do at home and it would be better if I had my own car."

"See you there." He clicked off without saying goodbye or ta-ta...or anything. I hated that—another strike against him.

Did etiquette say eat first, and then break things off, or should I deliver the bad news at the start of the evening? Crap, I'd have to ask Dee. She was always better at that stuff than either Brooke or me.

Dee answered on the first ring. "So, how was dinner? I thought I could wait for lunch to get the scoop, but my curiosity is killing me. Spill it."

"What makes you think there's a scoop?"

"Oh, darn." Her voice reflected her disappointment.

I grinned. I loved pulling her chain. "But I will confess that Zack sure knows how to kiss."

"Oh, yay," Dee said with a laugh. "Tell me more."

"I'm on a time crunch, so I have to cancel lunch with you today. Do you hate me?"

"No, but I'm disappointed."

"Well, what is it you want to talk about? I know we can get together tomorrow."

"I'm dating someone," Dee said. "I wanted to ask your opinion."

"Now, I'm intrigued and so pissed that I am slammed for time today. Do I know this guy?"

"I'd rather discuss it in person."

"Mysterious. Okay, here's an etiquette question. Pretend you were going to end things with a guy..."

"Uh-huh. You're dumping Richard. Good decision. Go on."

"And this guy was taking you to the Marble Mansion."

"*Ohhh*. Fancy. Food's great, by the way."

"What? You've been there?"

"Not why you called," she sang. "Continue with your scenario."

"Do I get to eat dinner and then break things off, or do I have to tell him before I get a juicy steak?"

"Whew. That's a tough one. Marble Mansion's got a fabulous filet mignon that melts in your mouth and is totally worth putting up with a douchebag like Richard to get one. On the other hand, I think you're required to do the right thing. I can see your problem."

"I don't get to eat, do I?"

Dee chuckled. "No. You have to tell him first.

Maybe a drink in the bar or at the table before ordering. That way, it's done and over. If he still wants to eat, order the filet mignon with crab. Delicious."

"Who did you go to the Marble Mansion with?"

"Not talking about me. Let's stay focused. I suggest you drive your own car. Men get a little touchy when they get dumped."

"Yeah, I'd already decided to do that. At some point, you need to tell me who you dumped that left you stranded. I can't believe there's a story I don't know. Now, let's talk about clothes. What's the best breakup outfit?"

Later that evening, as I fastened my necklace, I studied Baxter sprawled out on my bed. I hated leaving him home alone, but I suspected I wouldn't be gone all that long. In my experience—limited though it may be—men like Richard Long did not take rejection well. Even a mild disagreement with one of his opinions would leave him annoyed. I was not looking forward to tonight. I strongly suspected I wouldn't be enjoying one of those mouth-watering steaks my sister had described. Oh well. This had to be done.

But at least I could be sure Baxter would be safe at my house with my state-of-the-art security system. I chuckled at my own thoughts. If anyone had told me that I would have a dog in my house, much less in my bed, I would have accused them of being on some

CYNTHIA D'ALBA

type of hallucinogen. And yet, here I stood, smiling at a tiny dog lying on his back with his legs wrapped in my thousand-count thread sheets. The little monster had grown on me. I was going to miss him when he went home.

While putting the posts of my diamond earrings into my ear lobes, my phone vibrated beside me. The caller ID read "ZACK!"

"Hey," I said on answering. "I guess you got the message about dinner tonight.

"I did, but tell me what's going on. Your message was a tad cryptic."

"I'm doing exactly what we talked about. Richard called today and insisted on dinner."

"Richard. Is this the guy you've been seeing but won't after today?" His voice was deep and gravelly. Shivers ran up and down her spine.

"You know his name," I chided. "And yes, Richard. I'm meeting him at the Marble Mansion in about an hour." I sighed. "I wish it were politically correct to dump him via text."

"Ouch. That's brutal. Promise me you'll never do that to me."

I smiled. "Now, that's a promise I can make."

"Why didn't you just call him up and tell him to take a hike? Or even ask him to come by your house for a drink and do this in private?"

"Because I know him. He's going to be furious... not that he's so attached to me that losing me will be a heartbreaking for him. It's mostly going to be damage to his ego. He likes to be the one who decides

122

when a relationship is over. In public, he will be conscientious about his reputation. He'll be the perfect gentleman." I shrugged even though only I could see my action in my mirror. "In private, well, his anger is more likely to emerge. I'd rather not deal with that."

Zack was quiet for a moment. "Do I need to be worried about this guy? I mean, he's never hit you or anything, has he? Because if he has, you're not going to meet with him in private or in public." The barely suppressed fury could be heard in his every word.

"Calm down, Captain America. I'd never let a man hit me. And if one did, you'd never find the body."

"Good. Now that you've got my blood pressure into dangerous territory, explain why a simple phone call won't suffice."

I sighed. "Richard isn't a bad guy. Not at all. He's just not the right guy for me. But we've been together long enough he deserves to be told in person. It'll be fine. I promise. I even suspect I'll be early if you still want to have dinner."

"Aww, Princess. I was calling to let you know I got called into work. I'm sorry. I hate it, but it's the job."

"I understand. I really do. Call me later?"

"I know what I'd rather do to you later."

"Oh yeah? Tell me more."

He then spent the next five minutes going into graphic detail about what he wanted to do to me as soon as we had any alone time. Damn him. I ended the call with wet panties and a throbbing core.

An hour later, I pulled my Benz up to the valet stand at Mable Mansion and stopped. I exited and handed over the key fob, warning the valet, "You might want to keep it close. I'm breaking it off with a guy, and I suspect he won't take it well, so I might be out faster than your usual customer." I handed the guy a fifty-dollar bill. "Sorry to be a problem."

He pocketed the bill with, "Not going to be a problem for me." He winked at me. "I'll keep the getaway car close."

I chuckled and headed inside. At the reservation stand, I said, "I'm meeting Richard Long. I'm sure he's already here."

"Ah, yes. Ms. Carmichael. He mentioned he'd be meeting you when he made the reservation. If you'll follow me, please."

I silently laughed. The creep had used my name to get the reservation. It *was* who he knew, after all, and the *who* he knew was me.

Hanging crystal chandeliers provided subtle lighting to the room. Rainbow colors splashed on the walls from the pendeloques. Fresh flowers and globed candles adorned the white-clothed tables. Each table sported fine china, crystal stemware, and heavy silverware. Classical music played quietly in the background. Tables were filled with elegantly dressed couples, although there were a few tables with foursomes seated. The Marble Mansion enforced a strict adults-only policy, and while I enjoyed children as much as the next childless female, I found I preferred this calm environment.

Richard stood as I approached the table. He was tall, dark-haired, and cut a dashing figure in his custom-made Italian wool suit. More than one female in the room let her gaze roam over his body. He did have a luscious body, all muscles and toned sinew. It wasn't his body that was the problem with Richard. It was his attitude...or maybe it was just me.

"Andrea, you look beautiful," he said, and gave me a peck on the cheek.

"Thank you." He held my chair as I slipped into it.

"Your waiter will be right with you," the hostess said.

"Can we have a drink before we order?" I asked. "I want to enjoy the atmosphere." Plus, a drink might give me the boost of courage I needed to get through the next few minutes.

"Certainly." He snapped his fingers at a passing waiter, and I winced. I found that to be so...classless and crass. "Can you send our waiter over?"

"Of course, sir."

"Richard," I admonished, "that was rude."

He sniffed in such a way as to let me know he was in the right and I was definitely in the wrong. "They work here, darling. Our waiter will want a good tip, so I expect good service."

I gave up. I'd found over the years that money made people feel more important in this world than they really were. Richard was one of these people.

Raised in a middle-class home, he'd gone to college and, financially, had done very well. At times, it seemed as though he had to let everyone know he had money. I'd grown up wealthy, and maybe I did take it for granted, but I sure didn't flaunt it, did I? I hoped not.

A middle-aged man attired in black slacks paired with a long-sleeved, white shirt stepped up to their table. A crisp, white apron was tied at his waist and covered his pants down to his knees.

"Good evening. I'm Paul, your waiter for this evening." He gestured to the man standing to his right. "This is Zack, your waiter-in-training." Paul then handed each of us a tall, leather-covered menu. "May I start you off with some drinks?"

"I'll have the Pappy Van Winkle, aged twenty-three years," Richard said, not waiting for me to give my order first. "Neat, ice in a separate glass."

I wondered if I was supposed to be impressed with his order, or if maybe he was trying to impress the waiter with that order. Another way to flash wealth, I supposed. I'd had Pappy Van Winkle bourbon of all vintage years, and yes, the twenty-three was rumored to be one of, if not *the* finest bourbons in world. I wondered if he had any idea of the cost of what he'd just ordered. That fine glass of bourbon would set him back close to three hundred dollars minimum. It crossed my mind that the bar could probably pour any top-shelf bourbon for Richard, and he'd never know the difference.

I bit my tongue. That wasn't nice and I was

disgusted with myself for my harsh thoughts. For all I knew, he might have developed an excellent bourbon palate in the three weeks since I'd seen him.

I glanced up at the waiter and his assistant ready to order my usual martini. I almost gasped when my gaze met the gaze of the waiter-in-training, and then I could barely contain my amusement. Zack Noles, attired in the restaurant's black slacks and white shirt uniform, stood solemnly beside Paul, the waiter. Zack was the waiter-in-training? Was he undercover, or— and this thought sprang to her mind—moonlighting as a waiter for extra money? Had renovating the Skaggs house taken more money than he'd planned?

Since he didn't have one of the foundation grants, I was going to make it my business to see that he got some financial help. I hated to think of him working two jobs.

"Madam? A drink?" Paul asked again.

"Oh, sorry. Dry, vodka martini made with Ciroc vodka."

Paul nodded. "Very good."

Paul and his assistant left.

Or was Zack here to keep an eye on me? Did he not trust me to break up with Richard? Pulling myself together, I glanced across to Richard. "How have you been? Gosh, it's been a while since our schedules meshed."

"Busy."

"Well, that's good then, right?" I took a sip of the iced water on the table.

"Always good. Can't have too much money, am I

right?" Richard said and smiled. "Of course, you know all about that."

My spine stiffened, but I bit my tongue. He thought way too much about my family's money. He didn't appear to notice his faux pax and continued to speak.

"You lived in Highland Park growing up, right? I've been thinking about getting a place there. I feel like I need to live in an area more reflective of my station in Dallas, you know? Of course, you know. I'm surprised you didn't get a house there yourself. I mean, I'm sure Carmichael Gardens holds a special place in your family's history, but the houses are all so, I don't know, dilapidated, right? Yours is great, though. You did a fabulous job with all the renovations, but with the market the way it is now, you should sell. You could probably double your investment," he smiled, "smart lady that you are."

Zack returned with our drinks, serving my vodka martini first, followed by setting Richard's bourbon, and then a glass of ice, in front of him.

"Can I answer any questions about the menu?" Zack asked, his tone neutral.

Richard waved him off. "Give us a few minutes. We'll order later."

Zack dipped his head and sneaked a wink at me. I hid my smile behind the rim of my glass.

After he stepped away, Richard lifted his glass toward me. "To us."

I gave him a tilt of my head and took a sip of my ice-cold drink. The vodka in my drink was made from distilled French grapes. The drink was refreshing on a warm, Dallas evening. Unlike his bourbon, I would know the difference if the wrong vodka was used.

"Now," Richard said, setting his glass on the table. "As I was saying, today is the perfect time to unload that monstrosity of a house. The real estate market has never been hotter. My agent told me I should act quickly as soon as I found a house in the right area."

I nodded. Had he always been so insufferable? So self-absorbed? Had I simply ignored it?

"I was talking with Barney the other day—you know, Barney, right? Barney Rothsman? Anyway, he was telling me that he'd picked up a new ski lodge in Vale for a song. But knowing Barney, it was an expensive song, am I right?" He laughed at his own joke.

"How's your family?" I asked, trying to direct the conversation away from money.

"They're fine. My folks are talking about retirement and traveling around the country in a motorhome. Is that not the most ridiculous thing you've ever heard? Why, I told them it sounded crazy. Driving everywhere? Why not fly?" He shook his head. "They told me the drive was the fun part. I swear, sometimes, I wonder if they're really my parents or if I'm adopted." He chuckled again. "Now, did you get a chance to mention the investment I told you about to your father?"

"Richard, as I've told you numerous times, I don't talk finances and investments with my folks. Dad has his own people he works with, people he's worked with for years. He'd not keen on changing horses in the middle of the stream."

Richard's face grew a little flushed. "But we're dating. Surely, he'd be interested in giving a slice of his investments to his daughter's significant other."

Significant other? Holy cow. I really had let this go on for too long.

He reached across the table and took my hand. "I was going to do this later during dessert, but this feels like the right time."

I eyed him warily as fire alarm bells clanged in my head. I could almost see the flashing red light blinking, *Danger, danger.*

"I know your family will warm up to me once they realize how much we mean to one another."

"Richard, we don't have anything to prove... to my family, or anyone else, for that matter. They've only met you the one time, and besides, I have something I want to talk about."

"Me, first," he said. "Please. I want to get this out." He chuckled nervously.

I sighed. I hated losing control of a conversation when I had something important to say. I knew what he was going to say. He was going to suggest a vacation with him, me, and all my family. It wasn't the first time he'd made that suggestion.

Now that I gave it some serious thought, a joint family vacation, including him, was such a bad idea. Dee would probably kill Richard while he slept... with Brooke's help. With Brooke being a doctor, I was sure they could make it look like an accident and never spend a day behind bars. Neither of my sisters liked Richard and they'd only met him once. With time, I was sure they would grow to really loathe him.

I took a long draw of courage from my martini glass.

"I think we should get engaged," Richard said.

"What?" I sputtered, choking on the liquid in my mouth. My heart stopped at his question. I dabbed at the droplets of martini I'd spewed on the table. I lowered my voice. "What? Are you insane? We've barely known each other for six months. Goodness, Richard, I haven't even seen you in three weeks."

He gave my hand a squeeze. "I know, but with a ring on your finger, and us house-hunting in Highland Park near your parents, I know your dad would want his soon-to-be son-in-law involved with the family investments. Think of how we could grow the family fortune and build it into a healthy nest egg for our children and grandchildren. We would have such a wonderful life. No more sitting in some figurehead of a job. You'd be the queen of Dallas society and all that that means. The parties. The social gatherings. The charitable organization fundraiser. And think of our children. We would have the most beautiful children, who would attend only the most prestigious schools. And—"

"Stop," I ordered, jerking my hand away. This daydream of his was so far from reality that I worried about his sanity. "I'm not going to marry you."

His face, which had been glowing with excitement, dimmed. His head tilted with a confused expression. "You're not?"

"No, I'm not. In fact...." I drained the rest of my martini. As soon as my empty glass hit the table, a fresh one was set in its place. I downed the glass of bravery and looked at Richard. "I'm sorry, Richard, but I came here tonight to end this...this...whatever this is we have. It's not working for me."

"But it could," he insisted. "We're great together."

I pulled my hand back when he tried to take it again.

"No. I came here to tell you that tonight. I don't feel we should continue to see each other. I don't feel the same way about you. I confess I am more than a little surprised by the marriage proposal. I had no idea you felt that way. We've never spoken of love. Nonetheless," I continued, "this is our last date. I won't be seeing you again."

His face, which had been flushed, now flamed an irate, mottled red. "Are you fucking kidding me? You're breaking up with me?" His voice was loud, easily drowning out the background music. "Me?" He stood so forcefully that his chair tipped backward. "You bitch."

He threw a hundred-dollar bill on the table. "You'll be sorry. You'll come crawling back, but you know what? I'll be long gone."

Our waiter and Zack hurried toward the table.

"Sir? Sir? Is everything all right?" Paul asked.

Richard shoved their waiter to the side and

stormed through the dining room. I lost sight of him when he stomped into the lobby toward the exit.

I sighed. "Well, that was a little more dramatic than I anticipated."

"Are you okay, ma'am?" Paul asked.

"Definitely okay." I handed Paul my black American Express card. "Keep the cash for yourself. Put the drinks on here."

"Thank you. I'll be right back." He took my card and walked away.

"You look snazzy," I said in a ribbing voice to Zack. When his face remained neutral, I sighed, "Thank you for the second martini tonight."

"Yes ma'am," he said. "I could see things weren't going well, and here at the Marble Mansion, we want our patrons to leave with good memories."

Such an odd comment, right? Definitely undercover.

"Well, I'm leaving with memories, that's for sure."

Paul returned with my card and I signed the slip.

"Good night, gentlemen."

I gathered my purse and headed for the door. Outside, the cute—and very young valet—had taken me at my word, or maybe it was my fifty-dollar tip, but my car was parked by the curb at the front door.

"Thank you," I said.

"I'm thinking the man who just left was your bad news to deliver?"

I shook my head. "He was." I could only imagine

how rude Richard had been to the valet. "I'm sorry if he said something rude to you."

He walked me the few steps to my car and opened my door. "Whatever the gentleman said does not reflect on you, just as I hope tonight's visit to the Marble Mansion will not reflect on your opinion of us. I hope your next visit goes better."

I slid behind the wheel. "Thank you."

Ten

I thought about waiting up for Zack, but his hours were unpredictable. He might be home by midnight, or it might be eight in the morning when he finally pulled into his drive. So, I removed my carefully applied makeup, put on my most comfortable yoga pants—which happened to also be my holiest—and an old University of Texas T-shirt that'd seen better days. My toes rejoiced when they left the toe-pinchers of my high heels in favor of a pair of soft, fluffy slippers.

My stomach let out a loud roar. Either I was hungry, or the dragon inside had awakened. I went with starved. If only I'd placed an order to go at the Marble Mansion, but did they even do takeout? Could I send one of those delivery services over to pick me up a juicy filet with crab? Probably not, and there was a better than fifty-fifty chance my meal would get "lost" on the way to my house. The next option was my kitchen. Sigh. Not the best of possible options.

Baxter and I headed down to my kitchen to check out what dinner possibilities we had. Not Baxter, of course. He had his dinner all ready to go. What scared me the most was that I was so hungry that even his dog chow smelled good. Yeah, I needed to feed the dragon and fast.

I stood at my open refrigerator door and surveyed my supplies. It held all the makings for a large chef salad, so I decided that was better than wrestling Baxter for his chow. After assembling a rather decent salad, if I said so myself, I headed to the sitting room, followed closely by my eight-pound shadow. I set my wine on the table along with my salad and hunted for the television remote. Scrolling through the channels, I stopped on a popular contemporary western and dug into my salad. The channel was streaming last season's episodes to get the audience excited about the upcoming new season. The storyline was romantic at times, frustrating at times, and violent often—sometimes all three in the same episode. At midnight, my eyes were scratchy and my legs stiff from sitting for four hours watching mindless television without moving.

Baxter had long since given up on the show and now lay snoring in the chair beside me. When I stroked down his head and spine, he stretched and yawned. He wasn't much on stimulating conversation, but no one could question what good company he was. Until this week, I'd never realized how much time I'd spent alone. Was I becoming a dog person? That was the last thing I'd expected.

Before heading to bed, I let the dog out into the backyard to do his business. While I waited on him, I walked over to my fence to check Lillian's house, just to make sure no lights were on or doors were standing open. If my gaze happened to drift across the street to see that Zack hadn't made it home yet, then it wasn't as if I were snooping. I was conducting a neighborhood watch, or that was my story, should I need one.

The tiny dog bounded back up on my deck and jumped. His jump height was about to my knees. I leaned over, picked him up and nuzzled his head, saying, "Guess it's just you and me tonight."

He licked my nose excitedly, which I took as confirmation that he had every intention of being my bed buddy tonight.

My sheets were soft and smelled fresh. I loved the day my cleaning team came and transformed my house. Everything sparkled from the sinks to the light bulbs. Usually, after a day like today, clean sheets and exhaustion would put my lights out in no time. Not so much tonight. The scene with Richard played over and over. How could I have let him down easier? He'd caught me completely off-guard with the marriage proposal. Love had never been expressed, and now that I thought about it, he hadn't professed his love tonight unless you meant his love for my family's money. That love was crystal clear. At least the way the night had gone at dinner, there was no way to misinterpret my message. We were done.

I tossed my clothes onto the chair in my bedroom and slipped between my sheets. I tossed and turned. No position was comfortable. The sheets were too hot, too cold, too floral smelling. Was that a lump in my mattress? Finally, sleep came but not easily.

My phone began ringing and vibrating on the table beside my bed. I sat up, completely awake, having flashbacks to the last time I'd gotten a middle-of-the-night call. Snatching up the phone, I looked at the screen and saw I had a text from Zack.

> Zack: Didn't want to call in case you were asleep. Are you asleep?

> Me: Not really. Kind of tossing and turning in bed. You home?

> Zack: I'm home. I'd like to see you, but it's late.

> Me: If I'm awake and you're awake, shouldn't we be awake together?

> Zack: [smiling face emoji] I'm at your front door.

I threw on my robe and ran down the stairs. After disengaging my alarm, I flung open the front door.

Still wearing his waiter-in-training clothes, Zack stood with his arms braced on the beam over my door. Deep lines of exhaustion were etched at the corners of his eyes and mouth, but to me, he was gorgeous. The second our gazes met a smile curved his lips.

"Come in, come in." I grabbed his hand and dragged him into my entryway.

He stepped into my foyer and closed the door behind him with his foot. Then he took my face between his hands and kissed me. The tingle started at my lips but then exploded through the rest of my body. The kiss invaded my soul, infiltrating every corner of every cell. A dull throb pulsed between my thighs.

"It was all I could do tonight not to kiss you on sight," he said as he placed kisses on the corners of my mouth.

"Less talk, more action," I said, taking his hand and pulling him toward the staircase. "I've been waiting for you for years."

While it was true we'd only reconnected this week, the thirteen-year separation evaporated at his kiss. He was the reason I'd never found love again. My soul had recognized what I'd refused to admit all those years ago. Zack was made for me.

He swung me into his arms. "Richard's gone?"

Strong arms encased my thighs. I wrapped my arms around his thick neck and praised the god of exercise, if such a deity exited.

"Gone."

"You're mine then. I'm not giving you up as easily as that fool did tonight. I won't walk away from you without a major protest. You've been warned."

I kissed his mouth and layered kisses on his cheeks. "Good to know."

He climbed my stairs to the upper hallway. "Which way?"

"End of the hall. Room on the right." He took a step and I said, "Wait. Alarm."

He chuckled as I punched in my code in the alarm panel in the hall. "I am a cop with a gun. I could protect you."

"I'm not expecting you to be wearing your firearm in about five minutes."

He grinned, and my heart did a serious loop-the-loop. Every bone in my body liquified, and I was thankful for his strong arms.

I'd left on only the bedside lamp, which cast the room in a flattering dimness. He closed my door with his foot and walked toward my bed. Slowly, he lowered my feet to the floor allowing my body to slide down his. Electricity sparked everywhere, setting off small bonfires throughout my body. As my toes touched the floor, he slipped his hands inside my robe.

"You're naked," he said, his voice deepening.

I smiled. "You noticed."

"I'm a cop. It's my job to notice important things." His words were growled out. His Adam's apple slid up and down with his swallow. "For example, I noticed your erect nipples the minute you opened the door."

"Excellent observation skills, Detective."

He untied the belt holding the silk robe on and pushed it off my shoulders. He groaned his appreciation. "Damn, woman. No one should look as good as you do."

Arousal flooded from me. His rough, sex-charged voice stroked me without touching me. I was going up in flames beneath his touches.

His mouth found mine in a long, deep kiss as his large, callused hands roamed freely, gliding over my hot flesh. Soon, his mouth followed the trail of his hands, lips and tongue gliding along the paths his fingers had already traveled.

Fire roared inside me. Lust roiled through me, seizing me in its powerful grip. My head fell back on my shoulders as his tongue circled my navel.

He dropped to his knees and buried his nose between my thighs. "Fuck, you smell so good." His tongue stroked between my legs. My bones dissolved even as a shiver racked me. "Nectar of the gods," he murmured.

I was beginning to wobble. I widened my stance in an attempt to remain standing upright, but my knees were threatening to give out at any moment. When his tongue dipped inside me, I groaned as my stomach flipped. My hips began to thrust without any conscious thought on my part. I just knew I needed to move.

"Fuck, Zack. More," I groaned out. I swayed toward him.

Putting his hand on my stomach, he gently lowered me to the edge of the bed, my legs hanging over the side and my feet on the floor. He wrapped his hands around my ankles and set my feet on his shoulders, spreading me wide for him.

I'd never felt so exposed while feeling so safe. Only he had the power to make me feel this way. No one else ever had. In my heart, I knew no one ever would.

He lapped the flat of his tongue through my swollen folds and around my erect clit.

"Oh my..." I groaned and pushed my feet against his broad shoulders reflexively. My stomach clenched and pulled. My thighs began to shake. The throbbing of my pussy became a demand for more. My hips jutted off the bed, shifting and lifting to meet his tongue. My only thought he was destroying me, but then he bit and sucked one of my enflamed lips, and I cried out in complete ecstasy. When he then moved back to my rigid clit and sucked hard, a storm lashed wild and free inside me.

"Oh God, I'm going to come," I cried out as a thick strand of tension coiled inside me, ready to explode.

"On my tongue," he demanded. "Come on my tongue. I need to taste you, have you."

My back ached, pressing my head firmly into the mattress. The tightly wound coil released, sending an electrical jolt through me again and again. White lights and bright lightning bolts danced behind my closed eyelids. A low, guttural groan vibrated my chest.

And then my legs went lax, falling to the side. It was only then that I realized I'd probably squeezed the crap out of his head with my thighs when I'd come.

I sighed with blessed contentment. "Thanks. I needed that." I scooted farther onto the bed and pulled my legs up. "Do all the waiters at the Marble Mansion provide delivery services?"

He laughed. "For you, it's only me."

I flicked my fingers at his clothes. "Off, off. I don't want to be the only one in my birthday suit."

With a smirk, he reached over his shoulders, grabbed a handful of shirt material, and jerked it over his head, pulling the sleeves inside out, as only a man can do. He tossed the material to the corner.

I grinned and knee-walked to the edge of the bed to unfasten his belt. Then, just to torture him a tad, I slowly unzipped his pants. I was careful not to catch his raging erection in the zipper's teeth. That'd kill both of our nights.

He brushed my hands away and hurriedly pushed his slacks and underwear to the floor while, at the same time, toeing off his shoes. An ankle holster had to be removed before he could get to his socks. Once the holster was secured on the dresser, both socks were flung to where his shirt lay.

"Is it crazy that I found watching you remove your gun and holster incredibly hot?" I reached out to wrap my fingers around his fully engorged cock, but he shifted his hips to move out of my reach.

He shook his head. "Can't take it. I'll explode if you land one finger on me."

I stuck out my bottom lip in a pout. "Just one lick?"

With a grin, he tossed a couple of condom packages on the bedside table. "Nope. One lick, and I'm a goner." He joined me on the bed as I scooted backward to make room.

"Only two condoms?" I asked with an arched brow. "Oh ye of little faith."

"I know where there's more. Of course, that means getting dressed to go across the street to my house. Wouldn't want to shock the neighbors by running bare-assed naked over there."

"I don't know. Lillian would probably have gotten a kick out of it."

He chuckled. "She would have loved it. Now, I believe you told me less talk, more action?"

I wiggled as he ran his hands up the outside of my legs to my waist then jerked me down the bed until I was flat on my back.

"Very smooth. Learn that in police academy?"

"NFL, now hush." He kissed his way up my body. His hands roamed freely over every inch of exposed skin.

I turned my fingers loose to glide over every square of his naked flesh covering hard muscles and tense sinew. I loved the crinkle of his thick chest hair between my fingers. I rolled on top of him to use that abrasive hair on my sensitive nipples.

He flipped me back over. His mouth latched onto one of my taut nipples, and he tugged. I arched when a bolt of pleasure shot from my nipple to my pussy, which was now aching for attention. I pushed my breast against his mouth with a pleased moan.

"Feels good. Don't stop," I said with a groan.

He moved his mouth to the other breast while continuing to pinch and fondle the first one. A wave of longing rushed through my veins. Leaving a trail of kisses, he worked his way up to my mouth and gave me a kiss that wiped my mind of any men since him. It was as if my memory contained only him—his touches, his kisses. He was the only man I wanted to remember.

I spread my legs in invitation to join me. He settled between my thighs on top of me.

"You're so beautiful," he said, looking deep into my eyes. "So fucking beautiful." He kissed me again, while sliding his cock through my wetness but not inside me.

I was dying for the fullness of him inside me, stretching me to my max. I arched my back and pressed my throbbing pussy against his rock-hard dick

"I need you inside me," I said and wrapped my legs around his hips.

He broke away only long enough to slide on protection. Then he pushed the head of his cock inside. My walls stretched to accommodate his girth. I groaned and rewrapped my legs tightly around his waist.

"More," I said. "I want it all."

He pushed further until he was fully seated and

then stopped. I felt full, my pussy extended to its limit.

"Give me a second, or I'll come on my first stroke." He looked at me, then brushed my hair off my face. "I've waited over a decade to be back inside you. I knew it would feel good. I didn't know it would feel like this."

I was suddenly swamped with emotion by his words. "Like what? Tell me." And I prayed he was on the same wavelength as me.

He pulled back and thrust into me again. "Like heaven. Like coming home after a long time away. Happy." He thrust again. "So damn happy to be alive and with you."

My heart swelled as my breath faltered. Tears rimmed the bottoms of my eyes. He filled me with joy. A joy so pure I couldn't hold back the strong emotions coursing through me. I held him in my arms and let the storm whipping inside me grow until I was overcome. I came with his name on my lips.

He followed me and found his own release. My name was the one on his lips as he pressed his mouth to my temple.

We fell asleep wrapped in each other's arms, too sated and exhausted to stay awake.

The ringing of Zack's phone jarred us both awake.

"Dammit," he growled and crawled out of bed toward his pants. "Noles," he snapped into the phone. "Yeah. Yeah. Got it. I'll be there. I said, I'm coming." He clicked off his phone with, "Fuck."

"Have to go?" I propped up on my elbow and watched him as he hurriedly got dressed in the dark. I reached over and clicked on the lamp.

"Sorry," he said as he zipped his pants.

"Yeah, I'm sorry you're leaving, too. You stay safe."

He stopped dressing and walked over to the bed to sit next to me. "I've been waiting all my life for you. I plan to spend more days and nights with you. You bet I'll be careful."

I smiled and leaned over to kiss his mouth. "Remember, you're my cop now. Take care of my property."

He kissed me back. "Always. I'll talk to you later. One of us needs to turn the alarm off."

"Code is 11185. Reset it when you leave, okay?" I yawned and stretched. "What time is it?"

"Five."

I tossed the covers off with a sigh. He stroked my naked flesh with a hot gaze.

"I might as well get up. It's almost time anyway. And stop looking at me like that. Neither of us will leave the house today, and I have to. I've got lunch with Dee, and I've already canceled lunch already a couple of times, so that's not an option. However, lunch with my sister means I'll lose a couple of hours of work time." Standing, I stretched my arms over my head, then bent at the waist, pressing my hands flat on the hardwood floor.

"That's not playing fair," Zack said.

Still in my bent position with my ass high in the air, I turned my head to look up at him. "Just trying to give you a reason to come back tonight."

He roughly pulled me up and into his arms with a jerk. The kiss he gave me was passionate and possessive, making my toes curl on the hardwood floor. Then, he set me on my feet, an arm's length away. "Stop it. I have to go."

I fluttered my eyelashes coquettishly. "I'm not doing anything."

His laugh was gravelly. "Right. I'll touch base when I can."

A few moments later, I heard the alarm chime off and then back on, followed by the slamming of my front door. Baxter yipped. "Me, too, Baxter. I think I might keep this one."

Later that day, I walked into the Island Salad House to meet Dee for lunch. My sister was already seated and waved me over to a four-person booth.

"You look...different," Dee said, studying my face. "New makeup? *No00*," she dragged out as she studied my face.

I felt the blush as it rolled up my neck to my cheeks.

"*Ohmygod*, you had sex," Dee said.

"Good God, Dee. Keep your voice down," I admonished. "Everyone having lunch doesn't need to know."

"I know it couldn't have been Richard, because you've only looked like this once before. You did it with the hot cop."

"How do I look?"

"Happy. Elated. Sated. Glowing. Need I go on?"

I dipped my head. "No, I think you've said enough."

Dee reached across the table and grabbed my hand. "I'm so happy for you."

"Are you? Why?"

"Richard was a total prick. All he ever wanted to talk about was money, money, money. And Lord, I was always embarrassed when I was with you guys and he started flashing hundred-dollar bills around. No class at all. Now, Zack? I've always liked that guy. I talked to Brooke the other night about him, and once again, she said the entire female hospital staff was in love with him."

"Wait. You and Brooke have been discussing my love life?"

"Sure," she said unapologetically. "Who's got Baxter right now? Surely Lillian isn't home yet."

"He's with my office staff. I've forgotten whose day it is to pamper him." I rolled my eyes. "I'm afraid Lillian will be getting back a very spoiled dog."

Dee laughed. "Isn't that what a tiny dog is for? To spoil?"

"If so, I'm doing a bang-up job."

Our server came and we placed drink orders—iced teas for both of us. The waitress said she'd be right back with our drinks and then take our orders.

"So, you called this meeting," I said, nibbling on a saltine cracker from the basket on the table. "What's up?"

Dee nervously shifted her fork and knife around on the tablecloth. Then, she took a long gulp of water. Her cheeks grew red, as did her bottom lip, which she continued to chew on.

"Just spit it out. It can't be that bad. Did you lose your entire trust fund in some crypto-currency scam? Or are there nude pictures of you on the internet? What?"

"I'm dating a guy," she blurted out.

I blinked and nodded. "Cool. Is something wrong with him?"

Dee sighed and waved her hand. A tall, handsome man with dark hair and a chiseled, familiar chin walked over to our booth. Dee scooted over and the man slid in.

I leaned back against the booth's padded leather, in a slight state of shock. "Henry Thaxton."

Henry, my old boyfriend from college. We'd never been "get married" serious back then. He'd been fine to keep around when I'd needed a date or a night out. I'd actually liked the guy, but I'd always felt like he was as interested in my money as in me.

Since I knew neither of us had been hearing wedding bells, I'd been fine maintaining the status quo since I'd been out of Texas after our senior year for law school and he would not be coming with me.

However, he'd broken up with me during our senior year right before my birthday. That had been his pattern since we'd met as Freshmen. When a birthday, Christmas, Valentine's Day or any time he might've been required to drop some serious money on his "girlfriend," he'd done the disappearing act. I hadn't really cared much. Plus, it had only been after he'd broken up with me that I met Zack. Maybe, I should be thankful for his unintended assistance in my love life.

Still, I didn't harbor any ill will or romantic feelings toward him. Mostly, I felt neutral about him. However, seeing him again, and with my sister, gave me a little shock. I confess, it did cross my mind if he was replacing me with my sister. I'd reserve my opinion until I knew more.

But if he was serious about Dee, and treated her like she deserved to be treated, and he made her happy, I sure wasn't going to stand in their way.

"I go by Hank now," Henry, aka Hank, said as he draped his arm over the back of the booth and, by proxy, around my sister.

I nodded. "Okay, Hank." I waved my hand toward them. "Someone want to tell me what's going on?"

"Hank's selling real estate," Dee began.

"Uh-huh. And?"

"I saw how much you loved having your own house, so I decided I wanted to look around. Hank had the listing for a house I was interested in seeing. I had no idea that Hank Thaxton was Henry from college."

"Okay," I drawled out.

"He ended up showing me at least twenty different houses, and, um, one thing led to another, and he asked me to dinner. I didn't say anything to you because, well, frankly, it wasn't your business and..." She glanced over at him and back to me. "I didn't know if dinner was just a one-time meal or if there'd be others." She gave a self-conscious shrug. "There were more."

"You do realize she's my sister, Hank, and we look alike?" I said to Hank.

"First, of course, I know she's your sister. Well, I knew the minute she showed up for the house viewing appointment and walked in the door. And second, you are not identical. Oh, you look enough alike that some people might not see the differences, but I do. Her eyes are a different color. Her hairline is lower. Her ears are—"

"Yeah, okay," I said. "I get the picture. You've studied her. So, why are we having this meet and greet today?"

Dee took his hand. "It's more than dating, Andi." She glanced toward Hank, who met her gaze with such a loving expression, I felt like I was intruding on a private moment meant just for them. Dee turned her gaze back to me. "I love him."

"And I love her," Hank said.

"I didn't want you to think we snuck around behind your back or anything. It just happened."

I smiled and I hoped my expression looked more confident than I felt. "I'm happy for you...for both of you. You know I only want the best for you, Dee."

"So, you're not upset?" Dee asked, her top teeth gnawing on her bottom lip.

"Upset? Gosh, no. Not at all. I don't know what Hank told you about us, but we were never in love or talking long-term or anything." I leaned closer and lowered my voice. "We never slept together, Dee. I think we were more comfortable as friends than lovers."

"See?" Hank said. "Isn't that what I said?"

"I know, honey, but guys are, well, clueless sometimes when it comes to women's feelings."

"I have no feelings for him, Dee...well, except friend feelings. So, as far as I'm concerned, go forth and be together," I said.

Hank pulled a ring box from his coat pocket and turned to Dee. "You heard her. Go forth and be together. I can't imagine my life without you in it. I don't want to imagine my life without you. Will you marry me?"

My eyes popped wide open. I had not seen this coming. My vision suddenly blurred. Damned allergies. I used my napkin to dab at the corners of my eyes and sniffed.

Dee's mouth fell open and tears began rolling down her cheeks as she said, "Yes, yes, oh, yes." She threw her arms around his neck. "Of course, I'll marry you."

As he was slipping a ring with a diamond the size of Lake Ray Hubbard on her finger, I thought that he must really be doing well selling real estate since he came from a middle-class family and had no family money to pull from, or at least not to my knowledge. My phone began to ring and I thought seriously about not answering, except it might be Zack. I glanced at the caller ID and my heart skipped a few beats. The caller was my assistant, who never called while I was out of the office unless a situation had arisen that was so serious, she couldn't handle it. I knew it this was something major

"Excuse me," I said to the beaming and crying couple. "I have to take this. Hello? What's wrong, Robin?"

"It's Baxter. He's been stolen."

Eleven

$\sim$

"What? When? How?" My heart was racing. Blood pounded in my ears so loudly I could barely hear Robin.

"Heather took him down for his potty time and a man pulled a gun on her, demanding she hand over the dog. She was terrified. He grabbed Baxter and ran."

"You've called the police, right?"

My question, although asked quietly, still drew the attention of Dee and Hank.

"Yes, of course, but I don't know how serious 9-1-1 takes a dognapping."

I slid from the booth. "I'm on my way back. I'll call Zack on the way." I rushed toward the exit, only to find Dee rushing alongside me.

"I'm coming," Dee said. "And don't argue. We don't have time. That dog is worth a lot of money."

While we waited for the valet to bring my car, I phoned Zack.

"Hey, babe. Bad timing. Can I call you back?"

"No. Baxter's been stolen," I blurted into the phone and gasped against my tears.

"What? Did you call 9-1-1?"

"Of course, but you know where a dognapping will fall in importance on the crime scale."

My car pulled up. I handed the valet a twenty and slid behind the wheel. Dee jumped into the passenger seat. Both of us clicked our seat belts, and I tore out of the parking lot. I could afford any speeding ticket I got.

"I'll send a patrol car over to your office right now," Zack was saying over my car speakers as my phone linked. "Let me see if I can shake loose and get over there."

"Please hurry," I said as I took a sharp corner, almost hitting a parked car. "I need you."

"I'll be there," he promised and clicked off.

The ten-minute drive to my office felt like an hour. The palms of my hands were wet from sweat while perspiration rolled down my head and neck. My heart raced violently. My breaths were pants of fear. What was I going to tell Lillian? How would I find Baxter? This was horrible.

Dee hung on to the car's grab bar, not saying a word through the wild, highspeed race through downtown Dallas streets.

I flew into the circle drive of our office building and threw the car into park. I jumped from the car and ran for the elevator. As I anxiously waited, a patrol car turned into the drive, its lights flashing and siren sounding, followed by a nondescript sedan with flashing lights in its grill.

To my surprise, Zack exited the driver's seat of the undercover police car and rushed for the doors. The elevator doors slid open and I held doors open to allow Zack and the patrol officer to join me and Dee.

"What do you know?" I asked Zack.

"Nothing more than you told me."

Tears welled in my eyes. He put his arm around me and pulled me tight against him. "Don't cry, honey. We'll find him. I promise."

The doors opened on the top floor. I slipped from under Zack's arm and rushed out. "Robin," I called down the hall.

"We're in your office," Robin's voice called back.

In my office, Heather sat on my sofa, Robin sitting beside her, holding the hysterical woman in her arms.

"I'm so sorry, Andi," Heather blubbered. "I'm so sorry. I didn't know what to do. He had a gun."

"Oh, Heather," I said, dropping to my knees in front of the sofa. "You had to give him the dog. You had no choice. What did the guy look like?"

"Like this?" Zack asked, pulling out his phone and holding it up so Heather could see.

"Yes! That's him. He had a gun," she repeated, falling back into Robin's embrace and wailing loudly.

I grabbed Zack's phone and looked at it. "Fuck. Randall Branson. Why does he want this dog so badly?"

"I can answer that," Dee said, speaking for the

first time since they left the restaurant. "Baxter is worth five million dollars."

"*What!?*" I said, whipping toward my sister.

"Lillian left money for the person who inherits Baxter to make sure he lives in luxury and is never mistreated, just in case he outlives Lillian. The rest of her estate has been designed as a trust foundation for animal rescue that goes into effect upon her death."

"She left her grandson nothing?" Zack asked.

"That's right. She addresses why in her trust, but I don't think that's important—the why, I mean. Just that she didn't."

"That's probably what he tore the house apart looking for," I said. "Lillian's will or trust."

"I bet he found it, too," Zack said. "He knows the dog gets money, and he doesn't."

"That must really have pissed him off," I said. "But this plan to kidnap the dog is crazy. What is he thinking? Ransom?"

Zack shrugged. "Not clear, but let's be honest. He's not the sharpest tool in the shed."

"I hope you're right," I said.

Zack turned to the patrol officer. "This guy has been staying at the Red Bird Downtown Suites near the Cotton Bowl. Get dispatch to send a patrol car. Maybe he was stupid enough to take the dog there."

The patrolman nodded and walked away.

"I hate to say anything," Dee said, "but the money angle only goes into effect when Lillian is dead, and last I heard, my client is kicking ass in rehab."

Zack and I exchanged a glance. No words were needed. We raced into the hall.

"Stairs?" Zack asked headed toward a labeled exit door.

"No. Elevator is faster."

The elevator opened and we jumped in. I took Zack's hand for the minute ride down. Just touching him calmed my frayed nerves. As soon as the doors opened, we sprinted off toward my illegally parked car since his unmarked sedan was now blocked by a delivery truck.

"I need that park anywhere card," I reminded him as we ran.

"Yeah. I'll see what I can do. Give me your keys."

"Don't need them with me in the car. Key fob is in my pocket."

One press of the engine button, and my Mercedes sedan roared to life. Zack stomped on the accelerator, and the car shot from the drive. I hit the flashers, hoping other cars would see us and get out of the way.

As we neared the hospital, Zack badged a medical center security car cruising the area. The guy rolled down his window. "Emergency," Zack said.

We wheeled my Benz into the circle drive, led by the security car. We left the flashers going and ran for the entrance. The security officer was right on our heels as they passed through the lobby's sliding doors.

"You want to tell me what's going on?" the hospital security guard asked.

"We think a patient may be in danger. We don't

want you to call up and alert the staff. If the guy is up there, I don't want him to be spooked by the staff acting strange."

"Look, we have to warn the staff to stay out of the way."

Zack gave a crisp nod and the security guard used his radio.

Security commandeered an elevator and the three of us boarded. The climb to the eighth floor felt like an hour. Finally, the doors opened. Zack's phone rang. One glance at the readout and he answered, waving the others to stop.

I danced in place as Zack took his call.

"Noles. Yeah?" When he chuckled, I stared in disbelief that he could laugh right now. "Dog's okay? Great. Thanks, Bristol. Beers on me tonight." Zack gave me a nod. "Baxter's fine. He was tied to a table in the hotel room where Randall has been staying. Bristol said there was blood in the bathroom, but didn't seem to come from Baxter. He thinks Baxter must have bit Randall." He snickered again. "Couldn't happen to a better person."

"So, they have Randall in custody?" I blew out a breath of relief.

"Not yet."

"Damn," I muttered. "Why not?"

"He had a partner. A woman. Name's Wendy Watson. She told the patrol officer who arrested her that Randall had gone to the store for bandages. The cops are there waiting for his return."

I sagged against the wall. "Thank goodness.

Whew," I said on a long exhale. "I want to drop by and see Lillian while I'm here. Okay?"

"Sure. I'll be there in a minute. I want to touch base with the precinct on my other case."

"Don't hurry. I'll be with Lillian until you're ready to go."

Zack pulled out his phone and made a call.

The security guard caught the elevator back down to the lobby.

It took a couple of minutes before I found Lillian's room. Her door was shut. I didn't want to wake her if she was sleeping, so I eased the door open quietly to sneak a peek. I knew rehab was tough and would be even tougher on a woman Lillian's age.

The scene I observed was beyond believable. "What the fuck?" I yelled. "What the hell are you doing, asshole?"

Inside the room, Randall stood at Lillian's bedside. He had a pillow pressed firmly over her face. Lillian's limbs were thrashing as she struggled to fight him off.

"Zack, help," I screamed down the hall and rushed into the room. "Get off her, Randall. It's over."

"My own grandmother," he shouted, still holding the pillow over Lillian's face. "My own grandmother would rather I fail than give me the money I need."

I dug my hard, sharp fingernails into Randall's closest forearm and pulled.

"Get off me, bitch," he said, jerking his arm away.

I glanced around for something to use as a

weapon. He was going to kill Lillian if I didn't do something and fast. My gaze landed on a vase of roses. I snatched up the vase, lifted it over my head—pouring water down my back in the process—and hit Randall's head with all my might. The vase shattered. Large chunks of glass fell to the floor, along with Randall.

He dropped to his knees, the motion pulling the pillow off Lillian's face. Blood dripped down both sides of his face.

"You stupid, stupid bitch," he snarled as he struggled to stand. "I'm going to fucking rip your head off your body." He reached for me, murderous hatred in his eyes.

A loud blast tore through the open doorway. Randall flew backward, landing in the room's recliner. Blood poured from his chest. His mouth gaped open, moving like a fish out of water. And then, he stopped breathing.

I rushed over to Lillian. "Lillian, are you okay? Can you speak?"

Lillian was drawing in deep gasps of air. "I'm okay," she squeaked out. "Are you okay?"

"I'm okay," I said, tears streaming down my face.

Zack stepped through the door into the room, his pistol pointed toward the floor. "Nobody tries to kill women I adore," he said with a growl.

It took a couple of weeks for the shooting to be ruled justified. Both Lillian and I had no trouble testifying to our fear that Randall was going to kill one, or both of us.

Randall's girlfriend, Wendy, gave the police all the information they needed to close the case. Randall was in debt to some bad guys out of Las Vegas. Drug and gambling debts. Wendy testified that she'd only arrived in Dallas the previous night, so she'd had no idea that Baxter had been dognapped. Randall had told her to watch his grandmother's dog.

However, her story didn't hold up under Zack's interrogation. Wendy had been the second person involved in robbing Lillian's house. It took a while, but Zack was able to find the storage building where Randall had stashed the sterling silver pieces, the *objets d'art*, and some of Lillian's jewelry. The cash from her safe was long gone, used to pay Randall and Wendy's living expenses. But Lillian was more than happy to part with a thousand dollars if it meant getting her precious Baxter back.

Lillian came home two weeks after the attempt on her life. Zack and I brought over dinner and Baxter to welcome her home.

"Baxter," she cried and swept her dog into her arms. Baxter wiggled happily in her arms while covering every inch of her face with excited licks.

"I think you were missed," I said.

"I missed him, too," Lillian said. "Thank you, well, for everything. I never dreamed Randall was so... so evil."

"I think he was more desperate than evil," Zack said as he walked in from the kitchen. "Drugs and gambling are the evil elements that got hold of your grandson. I'm sorry for how it ended."

Lillian carried Baxter over to where Zack stood. She stood on her tip-toes to kiss his cheek. "You have nothing to be sorry for. I lost my grandson years ago. When he didn't come home for his own mother's funeral, I accepted I'd never see him again." Her face turned sad. "When he turned up here at my house, I'd hoped he was home, that he'd changed, but, well, you know how that turned out."

"You tried to help him," I said. "You tried to protect him."

Lillian sighed. "I did try." She pushed a smile on her lips. "I'm starving. What's for dinner?"

"Steaks, courtesy of the Marble Mansion, along with garlic mashed potatoes, toasted almond green beans, and fresh-baked bread." Zack grinned at the astonished expressions as Lillian and I exchanged looks.

"I swear, I've been wondering if they did take-out," I said.

"They don't," Zack said. "But they did it as a special thank you to me. Come on, ladies. Your table awaits."

"Zack's been practicing being a waiter," I confided to Lillian. "Maybe he has a career in the hospitality field.

Lillian giggled. "I can't wait to hear this story," she said, carrying Baxter along to the table.

Over dinner, Zack told the ladies that he'd acci-dentally stumbled on an employee stealing Wagyu steaks from the Marble Mansion to the tune of almost twenty-thousand dollars.

"The retail for Wagyu is about one-hundred-twenty to one-hundred-fifty dollars a pound. One of the teenage busboys thought he'd hit a gold mine. He was selling steaks out of the back door to his teachers and friends of his parents. Dumb ass."

"When did you have time to uncover this serious crime?"

"I think you know. I caught him pocketing the cash and delivering the product."

"How much do you think he stole?"

"Thousands, but I turned the case over to robbery and let them take it from there. Kid's facing some serious consequences."

While we'd been talking, I cut into my steak and my mouth dropped in shock. "Holy cow. This is like cutting soft butter with a hot knife." I put a piece in my mouth and moaned. "*Ohmygod*," I said with my mouth full. "I'll never be able to eat regular beef again."

"Sorry, honey, but on a cop's salary, it's hamburger."

I smiled. "Luckily, I love hamburger."

And if it meant having Zack in my life, I'd eat hamburger every day of the week but I also knew he was full of bull. He had a seriously nice nest egg from his NFL years, so a Marble Mansion steak was certainly within his budget.

As I enjoyed my meal, I listened in on Lillian and Zack's conversation about her garden and what she might plant this year. He was assuring he that he'd be happy to help.

I leaned back in my chair and watched the love of my life as he laughed and talked with my elderly neighbor. I'd never stop loving the twinkle in his gorgeous gray eyes or the way he made me feel just by holding my hand,

My heart was so full of love and joy that I couldn't suppress my smile. Years of separation and a lot of growing up and maturing had to happen to both of us before fate brought us back together. But I knew in my soul we would have a lifetime of love and happiness ahead of us.

Twelve

hree Months Later

"Damn, woman. Are you trying to screw me to death?" Zack said with a huff. "We do have the rest of our lives to do this."

I laughed and rested my head on his naked chest. "Well, I wasn't trying to kill you, but we do have all those years to make up for."

He chuckled, my head bouncing on his body with his laughter. "I don't think we have to do all those missed sex opportunities in the first year. Hey, I meant to tell you something." He stroked my hair, running his palm over my head and down my back.

"Oh, yeah, what?"

"I got an offer on my house."

I sat upright. "On the Skaggs house?"

"That's right."

"I didn't know you even had it on the market."

"I don't. I didn't. I was contacted by a real estate

agent last night with a client wanting to buy the house."

"But they haven't even seen it, right? You still have so much to do on the rehab."

"Princess, since you blasted back into my life, I don't think I've hit one nail or laid one tile at my house. In fact, I can't remember the last time I slept in my own bed."

"I know," I said guiltily. I snuggled down in the sheets next to him. "I'm so selfish. It's okay. You can go ahead and say it. I want you all to myself. So there, I've said it for you."

He chuckled again and then leaned down to kiss the top of my head. "I like your selfishness. You haven't seen me fighting it. Hell, Andi, all I have left in my house are a few pieces of bedroom furniture, my tools, and some renovation supplies. Most of my clothes have already migrated to your closet."

"You don't have enough clothes," I scolded. "You barely take up any space at all here." I sat up with a smile. "I know. Let's go shopping for you."

He groaned. "Let's not."

"You kill all my fun," I groused and cuddled closer.

"All your fun?" he asked in a dry tone.

"Well, maybe not all of it." I traced a finger around one flat nipple.

"So, back to the offer. Do you think I should consider it? I know you're working hard to rebuild this community into a family-centric neighborhood."

"What do you know about the buyers?"

"Engaged couple. Love the area. It seems like they're dedicated to restoring my house to its former glory. No kids. The agent mentioned maybe a dog, but definitely no children right now."

"Young couple?"

"About our age, I'd guess."

"*Ohhh*, it would be nice to have neighbors close to our age, don't you think?" I sat up again. "Wait. You're not thinking of moving somewhere else, are you?"

"You mean, sell my house and buy one in another neighborhood?"

I frowned. "That doesn't work for me at all. Here's what I think..."

He raised his eyebrows, a sight grin curving his mouth. "What's that?"

"If the price is right—and I mean you come out of the deal grinning like you robbed a bank and will definitely get away with it—then you move in here with me. Like you said, most of your clothes are here anyway. Plenty of room for your tools." I frowned. "Not sure about the bedroom furniture." While I would never say anything to hurt his feelings, his bedroom suite was cheap, old, and barely hanging in.

He laughed. "Yeah, that bedroom furniture has to go."

I breathed a sigh of relief. Tough subject successfully avoided.

"So, where's the downside? I get you to my selfish self, and you get a wad of money for a house that two other people are going to rehab."

He was quiet for a minute. "I love you, Andi. You know that, right?"

"I do know that. I love you, too. I don't want to spend a day without you in it."

"That sounded like a marriage proposal," he said.

My heart leapt into my throat and lodged there. I grew quiet. "Is that what you want? To marry me?"

They faced each other in the bed.

"If you'll have me, then yes. I know you're too good for me, and I'm lucky you ever gave this mug of mine a chance. I'll go to my grave loving you, so yeah. That's what I want," Zack said. "I want to marry you."

"Whew," I said, wiping the back of my hand over my brow. "Gosh, I've never proposed before. That's scary." The tension in the room popped when he laughed.

He pulled me in for a kiss. "I've never been proposed to before. Propositioned by a few hookers during arrests, but that's totally different."

I giggled. "I should say so. Oh!" I clapped my hands together. "Ring shopping. That'll be more fun than clothes shopping."

He grinned. "You can have any ring that fits my budget, not yours."

"Honestly, I don't need a ring." She hugged him. "You're better than any old ring."

My doorbell chimed, and I groaned. "Ignore it. They'll go away."

The bell chimed again, followed by pounding on the front door.

"I don't think they're leaving," Zack said.

"Grrr. I'll get rid of whoever it is."

"Naw. It's almost five. We should get dressed for dinner at least."

"We could do naked fajitas...?"

"Never again. That sizzling meat made, uh, my meat a little nervous."

I was laughing as we got out of bed and threw on clothes. Meanwhile, the racket downstairs continued.

"Damn, whoever is there is persistent," I muttered. "Damn bad timing." I flung open the door. "What?"

Dee and Hank stood hand-in-hand on my front porch.

I frowned, "What are you doing here?"

"You're right on time," Zack said from behind me.

I turned and looked at him with a confused frown. "On time for what?"

"Your surprise. Come on in."

The two men shook hands, as Dee gave me a hug.

"Surprise," Dee said.

I cocked my head, my confusion deepening. "Well, I am that." I looked at Zack. "What's going on?"

"First, I'd like to introduce you to the buyers of the Skaggs Place."

I whirled toward my sister, my eyes widening. "You are the engaged couple buying Zack's place?"

"That would be us," Dee said, putting her arm around Hank.

"This is so awesome," I said, dancing around the foyer. When I passed Zack, I punched his arm. "You are horrible. You knew I'd love this." I whirled toward Dee again. "He's been hinting that he might move somewhere else."

Zack draped his arm around my shoulders. "She got so nervous, she proposed."

"Zack! You're not supposed to tell that."

Dee and Hank laughed while my face heated.

"Would it help if I brought you a present for your engagement?" Dee asked.

My frown returned. "I am so confused."

"I'll explain," Zack said. "These two were supposed to come over this afternoon after *I proposed* to you. They were bringing a cake and your present, which I do not see. Guys? Present? Cake?"

Hank got a sheepish look on his face. "Yeah, we got the cake like you asked, but the present ate it."

I looked at Zack and arched a brow. "My present ate my cake? What in the world have you done?"

Dee shrugged. "Backyard. It seemed the safest place."

I grabbed Zack's hand and pulled him through the house and into the backyard, where I promptly squealed with delight. A large, black puppy galumphed toward me, spilling over its feet on the way. On the dog's face was a smear of icing.

"You got me a dog," I said. "A very big dog."

"She's a rescue," Zack said. "The animal shelter said she's a six-month-old lab and golden retriever mix. I know you've been missing Baxter."

"Oh, Zack." I started crying and hugging him. "Thank you. She's beautiful. Does she have a name?"

"Not really," Zack said. "The pound has been calling her Belle."

I wrapped my arms around the dog's neck as the puppy slobbered all over me. "Oh, Belle, I love you so much. We are going to have so much fun."

"I think you did good, brother-in-law-to-be," Dee said.

"Thank you."

"Sorry about the cake," Hank said as he shook Zack's hand.

"No big deal. There's always cake."

"Show Andi what we got," Dee said to Hank.

He nodded and headed out through the fence gate.

I was sitting in the grass playing with Belle, the dog lying on her back with her legs in the air while I scratched her belly.

The fence gate squeaked seconds before a black streak shot through the yard.

"What was that?" I asked and then started laughing as another black dog ran over to greet Belle. "Who is this?" I asked as I rubbed the new dog.

"This is Bro, Belle's brother. I couldn't leave him at the pound, could I?" Dee said.

"*Nooo*," I replied rubbing the backs of both the quivering dogs. "Siblings have to be together." As I said the words, I looked up at my sister and burst into tears. "You're moving across the street."

She plopped down beside me and cried. "I am. I'm so happy."

"I am too," I blubbered.

"Brooke swears she's not leaving Millennium Towers," Dee said.

"We'll get her over here yet."

We threw our arms around each other while crying and laughing."

"I'm starving," I confessed while drying my tears with the hem of my shirt. "Busy afternoon...if you know what I mean."

Dee howled with laughter. "Let's send the guys for pizza. What do you think?"

"I think that sounds perfect," I said.

I smiled as I saw my future full of family meals and rowdy dogs. Children? Who knew? But whatever came my way, I knew Zack and the rest of my family would always be there, and there was nothing more I could ever want.

"C'mon, Belle. I'll race you and Bro to the back fence." I took off in a run, both dogs barking and racing past me.

My sister's laughter floated down from my deck.

I'm thinking that maybe Carmichael Gardens should be renamed Carmichael Heaven because I was surely in FHeaven on Earth.

About the Author

New York Times and USA Today Bestselling author Cynthia D'Alba started writing on a challenge from her husband in 2006 and discovered having imaginary sex with lots of hunky men was fun. She was born and raised in a small Arkansas town. After being gone for a number of years, she's thrilled to be making her home back in Arkansas living in a vine-covered cottage on the banks of an eight-thousand acre lake. When she's not reading or writing or plotting, she's doorman for her border collie, cook, housekeeper and chief bottle washer for her husband and slave to a noisy, messy parrot. She loves to chat online with friends and fans.

You can find her most days at one of the following online homes:

Website: cynthiadalba.com

Facebook:Facebook/cynthiadalba

Twitter:@cynthiadalba

Newsletter:NewsletterSign-Up

Or drop her a line at cynthiadalba@gmail.com

Or send snail mail to: Cynthia D'Alba PO Box 2116
Hot Springs, AR 71914

Other Books by Cynthia D'Alba

WHISPERING SPRINGS, TEXAS
Texas Two Step – The Prequel
Texas Two Step
Texas Tango
Texas Fandango
Texas Twist
Texas Hustle
Texas Bossa Nova
Texas Lullaby
Saddles and Soot
Texas Daze
A Texan's Touch
Texas Bombshell
Whispering Springs, Texas Volume One
Whispering Springs, Texas Volume Two
Whispering Springs, Texas Volume Three

DIAMOND LAKES, TEXAS
A Cowboy's Seduction
Hot SEAL, Cold Beer
Cadillac Cowboy
Texas Justice
Something's Burning

DALLAS DEBUTANTES

McCool Family Trilogy/Grizzly Bitterroot Ranch Crossover
Hot SEAL, Black Coffee
Christmas in His Arms

Snowy Montana Nights
Hot SEAL, Sweet and Spicy
Six Days and One Knight

Carmichael Family Triplets Trilogy (coming soon)
Hot Assets
Hot Ex
Hot Briefs

SEALs in Paradise
Hot SEAL, Alaskan Nights
Hot SEAL, Confirmed Bachelor
Hot SEAL, Secret Service
Hot SEAL, Labor Day
Hot SEAL, Girl Crush

Mason Security
Her Bodyguard
His Bodyguard
Mason Security Duet

Other Books
Backstage Pass

Here's a quick peek at the other books in the
Carmichael Trilogy

Hot Ex

BOOK 2, THE CARMICHAEL TRILOGY

Fate can be a hormonal bitch

Finding your fiancé in the arms of another woman is every woman's nightmare. I should know. It happened to me. Did I panic? Did I run crying from our house? Yes and yes. Did I fling myself into the arms of another man? Not exactly, but somehow Rex Dockery is always there, exactly where and when I need him...like now. Being with Rex was like riding a unicorn in the Kentucky Derby...a fantasy...a dream. But a girl's real life can't be a fantasy world forever, can it?

Thirteen years ago, I met the woman I knew I was going to marry, only she choose Harvard Law School instead me. Maybe I didn't exactly ask her to marry me, but she had to know how I felt. Women knew these things intuitively, didn't they? I dated and played the field while I played in the NHL. I've only been in Dallas two days when I find Claudia Carmicheal, the woman of my dreams, slumped outside my neighbor's door in tears. Who ever made her cry like this is going to meet the end of my fist.

Fate is a funny thing. One minute it's flinging couples to the opposite sides of the country and the next, it's trying to make up for the past by slamming them back together. Can a couple go back and recapture the lightning in the bottle from their college days or will seeing each other only open healed wounds? Is it ever too late to start again?

Hot Briefs

BOOK 3, THE CARMICHAEL TRILOGY

Two lovers on a crash course with reality.

Being an emergency department doctor means being a jack-of-all-trades and I love it. Sure, the hours are long, and cases can be demanding, and sleep is something relegated to other people, but I thrive in the environment...until that one case comes along that knocks my feet out from under me. After such a case, I need to escape...my life, my work, even my condo. I need to lose myself in the arms of a stranger, someone I'll never see again, someone who won't ask me questions about my job. Tonight is one of those nights. I see him in the hotel bar. Tall. Dark hair. Ridiculously beautiful. His suit fits like it was tailored specifically for him. When he laughs, angels sing. He's the one. One night and I'll be fine tomorrow.

Being the single father of a pre-teen girl means I have very few nights off parental duty. I don't mind. I adore my daughter, but it's been a while since I've had a date, and even longer since I've made love to a woman. I know a mistake when I see it, and taking the woman from the bar to a room in the hotel is a mistake, but I want her as badly as I want my next breath. I know who she is, but I don't tell her who I am. If she knew my secret, she would run, and I can't let her go. Not yet. Maybe, not ever.

One night wasn't enough for either of them, but their secrets, if exposed, will destroy both of them. The secrets tick like timebombs. It's only a matter of time. Two lovers find themselves on a crash course with reality.

Made in United States
Troutdale, OR
02/14/2024

17687853R00106